ANGEL OF MERCY

A DARK, MAFIA ROMANCE

AJME WILLIAMS

ABOUT THE AUTHOR

Ajme Williams writes emotional, angsty contemporary romance. All her books can be enjoyed as full length, standalone romances and are FREE to read in Kindle Unlimited .

Shadows of Redemption Series

Soldier of Death | Queen of Misfortune | Prince of Darkness | Angel of Mercy

Mafia Mysteries

Tangled Loyalties | Savage Devotion | Bulletproof Baby

High Stakes
Bet On It | A Friendly Wager | Triple or Nothing | Press Your Luck

Heart of Hope Series
Our Last Chance | An Irish Affair | So Wrong | Imperfect Love | Eight Long Years | Friends to Lovers | The One and Only | Best Friend's Brother | Maybe It's Fate | Gone Too Far | Christmas with Brother's

Best Friend | Fighting for US | Against All Odds | Hoping to Score | Thankful for Us | The Vegas Bluff | 365 Days | Meant to Be | Mile High Baby | Silver Fox's Secret Baby | Snowed In with Best Friend's Dad | Secret Triplets for Christmas | Off-Limits Daddy

The Why Choose Haremland (Reverse Harem Series)
Protecting Their Princess | Protecting Her Secret | Unwrapping their Christmas Present | Cupid Strikes... 3 Times | Their Easter Bunny | SEAL Daddies Next Door | Naughty Lessons | See Me After Class

Billionaire Secrets
Twin Secrets | Just A Sham | Let's Start Over | The Baby Contract | Too Complicated

Dominant Bosses
His Rules | His Desires | His Needs | His Punishments | His Secret

Strong Brothers
Say Yes to Love | Giving In to Love | Wrong to Love You | Hate to Love You

Fake Marriage Series
Accidental Love | Accidental Baby | Accidental Affair | Accidental Meeting

Irresistible Billionaires
Admit You Miss Me | Admit You Love Me | Admit You Want Me | Admit You Need Me

Check out Ajme's full Amazon catalogue here.

Join her VIP NL here.

DESCRIPTION

Don't fall for a pretty face, they whisper.
Luca Conte, with his shadowed past, was a storm I couldn't resist.
He promised escape from a gilded cage, a future painted in
freedom.
Now, I'm his pawn in a ruthless game, my brother furious at my
betrayal.

Love burns bright, but his secrets choke the flames. Betrayal stings.
Luca's a house of cards, built on lies.
Can I escape the inferno before the whole world comes crashing
down?

PROLOGUE: LUCA

Two Weeks Ago

One lesson my father taught me when he was preparing me to take over as the Don of the Conte Family in Italy was that it was better and easier to ask for what you wanted than to simply take it.

Another tip he gave me was that politeness and charm made it easier to get what you want over threats and brute force. Not that he nor I weren't willing to kill for what we wanted, but such actions are messy and best avoided if they're not necessary.

The third lesson my father instilled in me was to always honor tradition.

Today, these lessons seem sexist and old-fashioned, but the Mafia is deeply rooted in those antiquated traditions.

I remind myself of these teachings as I stand before Don Niko Leone. He leans against Donovan Ricci's desk while the ladies have a baby shower in Donovan's back yard.

I like Niko and have a good working relationship with him. Killing him for what I want would not only be messy, but problematic. He is the single most powerful Don in New York. Hell, on the entire East Coast of the United States.

Not that I'm afraid of him. I'm powerful in my own right, even if I live an ocean away in Italy. But I'm not interested in waging a war if I can avoid it. Even so, make no mistake, I will get what I want from him one way or the other. And what I want is Niko's sister, Aria Leone.

I am hopeful that Niko will be reasonable, although he's known to be a hothead, and he doesn't stick to tradition as much as other Mafia Dons. I hope the latter facet of him will be to my advantage. But the way he crosses his arms and scowls at me suggests that he knows why I'm here and he doesn't like it.

I start by offering him the respect he deserves. "I appreciate the face-to-face meeting, Don Leone."

"If this is about Aria —"

"I've come out of respect to ask for her hand in marriage."

Niko's brows arch in surprise, and I'm wondering what he thought I was going to ask. Sure, my father bought Niko's sister-in-law, Lucia Fiori, from her father, so I suppose it's not out of the realm of possibility that I am looking at a similar arrangement.

But Aria isn't a woman a man buys like a side of beef. It's out of respect for her, not Niko, that I'm here asking for her hand.

From the moment I met her, I've known she is the one to be the queen of my Family.

It isn't just that she's a Mafia princess. It's not that she's obscenely beautiful and has a body that has ignited my fantasies. A body I have yet to touch anywhere except in my dreams.

It's not even that I know she understands our world and will be able to navigate it easily. It's her vibrant personality, her adventurous spirit. She's intelligent, although her sheltered life has made her slightly innocent of the world.

"Is she pregnant?" Niko asks.

His question offends me, not so much for me, but for Aria. "I respect you more than that, Don Leone. I have not touched her." Not that I don't want to. Not that I haven't had opportunities. But it's been clear to me that I need to play my hand right and treat her and her brother with the respect expected by Mafia Dons.

"I appreciate your showing me respect by coming in officially and making your offer—"

"But I haven't made my offer yet." I know we need to negotiate the arrangement. I must offer something to him in return for Aria's hand. To be honest, I feel I've already paid and Niko owes me. Niko has his happy home, as does his best friend, Donovan Ricci, because of my assistance in his war against Tiberius Abate and Giovanni Fiori, both of whom are now dead.

Plus, I would've been well within my right to force Lucia to come back to Italy with me. I promised my father that I'd take care of her when he died. Hell, I could've forced her to marry me, despite the fact that she had been married to my father.

As creepy as that sounds, my father never consummated the marriage. He and Lucia grew to love each other, but the marriage was completely platonic. My father had been too sick by the time he married her to have more than that.

My decision to let Lucia stay wasn't completely out of the kindness of my heart because I could see an alliance with Niko and Donovan would be beneficial to my black-market import-export business. But it had been knowing that Lucia had finally found happiness away from that fucking father of hers that persuaded me to let her stay. As such, I have already given more in this relationship with Niko than he's given me.

Even so, I'm prepared to offer him access to our black market trade into New York. There's no price I won't pay to make Aria Leone mine.

Niko holds up his hand to stop me. "There is nothing that you can offer me that will have me agreeing to your marrying my sister."

Anger simmers in my gut as his words feel disrespectful. He may be the most powerful Don in the eastern United States, but I am equally as powerful, if not more so.

The Mafia was born and bred in Italy. Niko Leone exists because of what my ancestors created. He isn't the only Don I have ties to in the United States. I know other Dons who would be eager to see Niko taken down a peg or two, or out altogether.

"I believe you owe me more resp—"

"I don't owe you shit—" Niko stops himself as if he recognizes his words can be taken as an act of war.

I suck in a breath, holding back the anger. It's clear that *il Soldato della Morte* believes the power and influence he holds means he can say no to me. But he has never met a Don like me, and he will discover that one way or another.

"It's not that I don't appreciate what you have done for my family, Don Conte. There are many ways I'm willing to repay you. But handing over my sister to you is not one of them."

I tilt my head, wondering what he possibly sees is wrong with me. Does he have the balls to tell me to my face? "To what do I owe this disdain from you, then?"

"I wouldn't call it disdain. Not yet, anyway."

"If you're concerned about how she'll be treated, you can rest assured that I am fond of Aria."

He lets out a scoff. "I'm sure you are. You don't think I know how people look at my sister?"

I clench my fists at my side, insulted at the way he would denigrate his sister. "You disrespect Aria with your words. I'm not looking for somebody to fuck, Don Leone. I assure you I can find that other ways—"

"Then why don't you?"

"Because I want Aria." I take a slight step forward, showing authority. I am no doormat that he will walk over. "I will have her. It's a good match, Niko. We are well-suited. And I know that she wants to be with me."

Niko straightens from where he's been leaning against the desk, asserting his own authority. "Aria doesn't know what she wants. She's too young—"

"She is nearly as old as your wife."

"That may be, but she's immature. Unworldly."

I stare at him, wondering where he's coming up with this? Yes, there's an innocence that comes from a sheltered life, but I can't say she is immature. "Didn't you have her living in Europe? Clearly, she's aware of the world."

"Not all of it."

"She'll never grow into the woman that she can be if you don't loosen your apron strings. At some point, she's going to do her own thing. You won't be able to control her forever."

"By her own thing, are you saying she wants to go from one gilded cage to another? Control of one man to another? If Aria has a passion she wants to pursue, I will support that."

My phone rings, and I inwardly curse at being interrupted. I glance at the caller ID in case it's something important. It's Bruno, my underboss.

I give a nod to Niko. "This is not over yet, Don Leone. But I have to take this call."

"As far as I'm concerned, this discussion is over."

I leave Niko, exiting Donovan's office and finding a quiet place in the foyer where I pick up my call from Bruno. It's late in Italy, so it must be important.

"Bruno."

"You need to get home soon, Boss," Bruno says to me in Italian. "Sabini thinks that when the cat's away, the mice can play."

Sabini has been a thorn in the Conte Family's side for generations, but Enzo Sabini has taken it to a new level, one that is going to get him killed if he continues to fuck with me.

"You can't handle it?" When I'm gone, Bruno has as much authority as I do, although admittedly, he may not be as ruthless at wielding it.

"You don't want them to think you're hiding or weak."

My jaw tightens. "I'll be home soon. I'll let you know when I'm on the plane."

When I return to Donovan's office, Niko is there with Donovan and the Bratva leader, Liam Rostova. It's odd to see him there, except for the fact that Liam was once Niko's consigliere.

"What have I missed?" I ask as I enter the office. Up until a moment ago, I've been friendly with the group.

Niko sneers at me. Donovan rolls his eyes, telling me he's aware of the situation and apparently thinks like I do. Niko is obsessively protective of Aria.

"We're toasting to Liam getting his shit straight with Kate," Donovan announces, handing me a drink.

"Hear, hear," Niko says.

"Congratulations." I join in, but I keep my eyes on Niko.

"How long are you in the U.S.?" Liam asks me.

"Not long. I have to return to Italy."

Donovan frowns. "I hope these visits aren't about checking on Lucy because as you can see, she's just fine."

I nod to him. "Lucia is very happy. I have no reason to check on her. Besides, she's a fierce woman who can take care of herself."

"Damn right." Donovan downs a shot.

"So, why are you here?" Niko's shrewd eyes narrow in on me. I wonder what he's getting at since I told him earlier. Or perhaps he's curious about my other activities in the United States.

"Business."

"What business?" Niko's hackles rise. Does he worry I'm working with a rival Family?

I set my glass down. "It's not one that concerns you, Don Leone. I value our alliance." I turn to Liam, shaking his hand. "Congratulations again. When love can blossom and grow, it's a lovely thing."

Then I shake Donovan's hand. "As always, it's a pleasure to see you and Lucia." Finally, I give my attention to Niko. "*Arrivederci*, Don Leone." I want to tell him again that this issue isn't over, but I don't want to ruin the celebration.

When I leave the office, I see Aria waiting for me. I give a quick shake of my head, not wanting to cause a commotion during a baby shower. I give her a signal to meet me outside and make my way out the door.

A few minutes later, she joins me by my car where my driver is waiting.

"I have to return to Italy," I say to her.

She pouts, and it's adorable. "Is my brother still being a dick?"

I nod, wondering if she's caught on to my plans for her. I haven't told her I want to marry her. The most we've done is discuss her coming to visit me in Italy. "Don't fret, *Mio Angelo*." I wonder if her Italian lessons have taught her my little pet name for her, *my angel*.

"When will you be back?"

"I'm sorry. I will be awhile." Being in touch with her will be a challenge. If Niko hasn't already blocked me from her phone, it will happen soon. An idea comes to me. "I think you should practice your Italian." I use my phone to research bookstores in Manhattan. I find one in the quaint East Village. "You should visit this store for more language books."

She arches a brow at me in confusion. "Why?"

"As I said, you need to learn more Italian." I lean forward and kiss her on the cheek. "*Ciao, Mio Angelo.*"

I have my driver take me from Donovan's in New Jersey to the East Village of Manhattan. I'm lucky the bookstore is still open. Going in, I find the language section. I slip a piece of paper between two books on the Italian language.

I exit the shop and tell my driver to take me to Teterboro Airport where my plane is waiting. On the flight back, I'm on the phone dealing with business even though it's the middle of the night in Italy.

When I land in Rome, I imagine that Niko thinks he has gotten rid of me. But he has not.

While my father advised me to do business as politely and respectfully as possible, he also told me never to be afraid of being ruthless and lethal if necessary. That's a lesson I've had much practice in, and I won't be afraid to follow it to make Aria mine.

1

ARIA

Current Day

I try to act nonchalantly as I descend the stairs and make my way to the front door of my brother's penthouse where I've been staying since my return to the United States nearly a year ago.

I wouldn't call myself a prisoner, but my brother's control is felt in nearly every aspect of my life. I'd much rather live on my own, but Niko won't allow it, at least not right now.

I swear to God he thinks I'm still sixteen years old. I do have the freedom to leave as long as I stay in Manhattan and I take along the bodyguards he's assigned to me. His watchful eye has been worse ever since he met with Luca in his office two weeks ago at Kate's baby shower.

I don't know what happened in that meeting. I only know that at the end of it, Luca returned to Italy.

Ever since then, I've been giving my brother the cold shoulder and silent treatment except in the few moments when I tell him what a jerk he is. Why does he get to have love and happily ever after, but not me? Not that I'm sure that's what Luca and I would have, but it's definitely possible. If only we could be together to find out.

I reach the elevator and press the button.

"Where are you off to today?"

Inwardly, I swear then turn around, giving my brother a sweet smile that he knows isn't sincere. "I'm going out." I turn to face the elevator again.

"Marco and Danny are with you, right?"

I raise my hand, giving him the bird. Niko accuses me of being immature, and maybe I am. But it's his fault. I'm certain that if I started acting like a fifty-year-old woman, he'd still keep close ties on me and wouldn't let me choose my own decisions in life.

The door opens and I step into the elevator. I turn to see Niko still standing at the door, his arms crossed over his chest, his eyes narrow, scrutinizing me.

I arch a brow, taunting him with the idea that he doesn't really know what I'm doing. And he doesn't. Even if Marco and Danny have told him about my regular trips to the East Village where I visit an excellent coffee café, play with kittens in a pet store, and peruse a bookstore, Niko would have no idea what that all means. I wouldn't put it past him to have sent men down to check out these establishments. But they won't find anything.

I make it down to the garage, and Marco holds the door open as I climb into the back of an SUV. He and Danny sit up front.

"To the coffee house?" Marco asks as he pulls the car up to the garage door, waiting for it to open to let us out.

"Yes, please."

"They must have the best coffee in town," Danny says. His tone suggests that Niko has asked them to see what they can find out about my outings.

"The almond croissants are to die for. They remind me of the ones I had in Paris." For several years, I lived in Europe, going to school and traveling. It sounds like fun, and it was, but Niko's presence was always felt. I was never without protection.

Traffic is heavy, so I settle back and take in the sights along the ride. New York is a lovely city in May. I wonder what it's like now where Luca lives, in Italy? Anger burns deep in my belly at the idea that I may never be able to find out. Stupid Niko.

My brother, Niko, took over the Abate crime Family's business, and with the help of Donovan and Lucy, the Fiori Family business in New York and New Jersey. For a long time, that meant everyone close to Niko had to stay home or at the compound, or go out with an army of men until his control was complete.

But now that things are calmed down, I'm allowed to go out with only two bodyguards and have enough freedom to go into a shop without their hovering over me. So, when we get to the coffee shop, Marco parks the SUV, and he and Danny escort me to the door.

This time, Marco stands outside while Danny enters with me, but once he scans the place for signs of danger, he goes to a seat in the corner, and I go to get my almond croissant and cappuccino.

I open my book on the Italian language and pretend to read. What I'm really doing is going over a note that I'm about to leave for Luca in the bookstore.

Two weeks ago, when Luca told me he had to leave but encouraged me to get some Italian language books, I didn't know what to think. What I hoped was that he was telling me to get better at speaking Italian because he would come back for me.

But when I went to the bookstore that he told me to visit, as I went through each of the Italian language books, a piece of paper fell out between two of them. When I opened it, my heart swelled.

Don't fret, Mio Angelo. *We will be together soon again.*

Mio Angelo. My angel. He calls me his angel. It makes me sigh each time he says it. He's such a romantic.

I stared at that note for a long time, feeling both happy and yet frustrated that this is what Niko has forced us into. Leaving secret notes. We can't text or call as Niko blocked Luca. And even if we could call, I wouldn't put it past Niko to listen in or record the conversation.

The notes are sweet and romantic, but they make me yearn even more to be with Luca. I have to somehow get to him. Luca is a generous, fascinating man. It's hard to believe he's a Mafia Don because he doesn't ever act like a beast like my brother does.

When I finish my coffee, I exit the café with Danny and Marco on my heels.

"I think I want to go see if they have any new kittens at the pet store."

Danny and Marco follow with enough distance to keep me safe without crowding me. I enter the little pet shop and go immediately to the pen where all the kitties are kept. Someday, I'm going to buy one or two and give them to my niece and nephew. With any luck, they will pee and poop all over Niko's penthouse. Petty and immature, I know, but again, it's Niko's fault.

It's times like this I wish my parents were still alive because I know for sure that they would think Luca is a good match for me. They wouldn't have hesitated to allow me to be with him to see if a marriage is possible. I wish I knew what is wrong with my brother that he is so against it. I've gotten to the point where I'm a little worried he's negotiating a marriage to somebody else in a business arrangement. The thought of it makes me sick.

I spend twenty minutes with the kittens and then exit the pet shop and continue down the street. "Wonder if there's any new books out this week." I've made this trip four previous times in the last two weeks, so Danny and Marco know the drill.

I go into the bookshop, and this time, Danny waits outside while Marco enters but stands near the counter flirting with the woman working there.

I make my way toward the back where the language books are. I pull my note from my purse, ready to make the exchange and read what Luca has left for me.

I know he's in Italy, so I'm not sure how these notes are showing up here. Part of me thinks that maybe he's enlisted Lucy's help. After all, she had been married to Luca's father until he died.

Plus, I know she thinks Niko is being unreasonable about Luca and she has no problems telling him so. But she has no power to help me. And I can't be sure that if it's not her helping Luca, that she wouldn't tell my brother.

I start going through the Italian language books, and there's the note. I quickly snatch it and look around to make sure Marco isn't watching, and then I open it, holding my breath as I wait to see what Luca has to say to me.

Mio Angelo, I miss you more than I can bear any longer. I am hopeful that your affection for me is still strong and you will come to me in Italy. Tonight.

I gasp at the message. Excitement and terror collide all at once. I love the idea of running away to the man I love. But I also know if I'm caught, Niko will lock me away and quite possibly hunt Luca down and kill him.

But there's also a little tiny bit of fear in going to Italy. I'm not as skilled in speaking the language as I should be. And what are Luca's intentions?

Living in a Mafia world, I'll never have the true freedom that other women enjoy. Leaving Niko and going to Luca means going from one controlling man to another. I might run away, but once I'm with Luca, I am his and under his control.

But then I think of his shy smile and his gentle gestures, like his fingers light on my back when we're walking. Stolen glances across the room when we're sure my brother isn't watching. One time, he acted as my bodyguard and whisked me away to a picnic on the river. We also went to Kate's bookstore that day, the first day I had bought a new language book. I wanted to learn his language because when he spoke Italian to me, my insides melted.

I fold up the note, shove it deep into my purse, and do my best to peruse the books while on the inside, I'm a kaleidoscope of emotions. Am I going to do this? Am I going to run away to Italy to be with Luca?

When I get back to the penthouse, I go immediately to my room and pull out the note again. On it, Luca has given me a date and a time—tonight, six p.m.—and a location, outside White Plains, to make my escape. He hasn't given me much time to decide, much less prepare, but maybe that's on purpose. If I have too long to think about it, there's a bigger chance of Niko finding out.

I grab my carry-on bag, too small for a trip to Europe, but I don't have a lot of time, and I'll need to sneak out, so I can't carry too much. I pack the basics and essentials and then hide the bag in my closet.

The next question is do I share my secret with anyone? Or do I leave a note? As much as I despise Niko right now, he has taken care of me since my parents died ten years ago. He is my brother, so it seems like I owe him something. But what would I say? Once he realizes I'm gone, he'll know where I've gone. And besides, leaving a note is risky. If he finds it before I'm away, he'll stop me.

I sit on the edge of the bed as I realize that in doing this, I am choosing Luca over my brother, and I hate that. But in the world that

I live in, it isn't just hatred and resentment that can build between Families. My running away to Luca could cause a war between our Families. Wars that end in death.

I let out an exasperated moan. Niko says I'm immature, but he's the one who decides conflicts can only be resolved with violence. Stupid macho man.

I continue to sit as the clock ticks away and the time frame for making my decision shortens. What do I do?

2

LUCA

I'm working in my home office along the coast of Civitavecchia. Well, I'm trying to work, but my thoughts are filled with Aria and whether or not she'll be on the plane tonight. I check my watch for the umpteenth time.

Just after nine p.m. Doing the math, I know it's only just after three in New York. Three hours before I know whether she's gotten on the plane. Does she want to get on the plane? And if she doesn't, is it because she's changed her mind about me or because Niko has found this out?

The idea that I might have put her in Niko's already overcontrolling crosshairs doesn't sit well. But what other choice do I have? As much as I want to be there to meet her at the plane in New York, I can't leave right now because I have to deal with Enzo Sabini and his fuckup antics.

I'm excited in a way I can't remember ever being except maybe as a kid. It's an odd feeling to be a ruthless businessman while at the same time feeling giddy about a woman.

Thinking of Aria in my home, in my bed, stirs me up. The arousal is made all the more painful because I haven't been with a woman in so fucking long. As many times as I've visited New York and seen Aria, I haven't touched her. All that I have available to me are my imagination and my hand.

At first, I found this situation to be embarrassing. I'm a man, after all. And while I was immediately drawn to Aria after a trip to New York four months ago, I began to second-guess her pull on me. Or maybe I was just in need of a good fuck.

So, I went to my club to see Electra, a woman I used to fuck regularly. She sat in my lap, running her nails down my chest, and my dick withered. And so, I've been waiting for this day for a long time. A day when I can make Aria mine in every way.

I consider going to the gym and working out the tension, but I know from experience that it won't work. This hard-on is here to stay until I jerk it off or Aria shows up.

But even if she's on that plane, she won't make it to the villa until tomorrow. And as much as I want her, I have to respect her. If she's not ready to take the relationship to the next level, I'll have to wait.

Wait? Fuck.

I'm no masochist, so I head to my bedroom, stripping off my clothes and stepping into the shower. If the gods are with me, this will be the last time I have to do this. Aria will be on the plane, and when she gets here, I'll be able to give up the fantasy to have the real thing.

The idea of it makes me even harder. I imagine her on her knees, that luscious mouth of hers wrapped around my dick. I stroke myself as I picture her dark eyes looking up at me with a blend of mischief and desire.

Or maybe we'll be in bed, her long, curvaceous legs wrapped around my hips as I sink my cock deep into her sweet pussy. I stroke again, the electric current crackling through my dick. I switch up the scene and she's riding me, bouncing up and down my dick, her round tits bouncing. My hand strokes like there's no tomorrow. All the images morph into one as my balls contract and my orgasm releases on a yell.

I press both hands against the wall and dunk my head under the shower as my breathing comes back under control.

What am I going to do if she's not on that plane?

I push that worry away. She'll be there. She has to be.

I get out of the shower and put on a robe, resisting the urge to call Bruno to see what's going on in New York. I'm not even sure she got the note. Maybe I should call my contact to see whether the note has been picked up.

I chastise myself for being such a pussy. The need for this woman is emasculating me. I'm not a man who sits around and waits for what he wants. I ask, and if I don't get it, I take it. My original plan had been to do just that. I would meet her at the bookstore and get her away from her bodyguards, then bring her here. But I've sent Bruno because Sabini is a fucking pain in my side and because I know Niko is on the lookout for me.

I suppose in some ways, this is a test because I don't just want Aria. I want her to want me too. I want her to grab life and go after what she wants. And yes, I want her to defy her brother. Oh, how I'd love to see the look on his face when he realizes Aria has left him for me. Assuming that's what she's done.

Unable to help myself, I check my watch. It's closing in on ten o'clock. If she's going to make it to the private airport on time, she's going to have to leave soon.

I slip on a pair of lounge pants underneath my robe and cross the hall from my room to the guestroom that I've asked Roberta, my house-keeper, to make up for Aria. The room is set up exactly as I think Aria will like it. Of course, there's all the comforts she would need in a bed, sitting area, and a large ensuite bath with an extra-deep tub to soak in. Imagining her wet and slick with soap makes my dick twitch again.

But the decor is also what I believe will fit Aria's style. It has a four-poster bed, and rich, colorful tapestries illustrating the history of my Family in Italy adorn the walls. A plush chaise lounge sits near the window, perfect for a Mafia princess to lounge in. As much as I hope she likes the room, what I really want is for her to move into my room. Small steps.

Determining that everything is set, I exit and head back to my office downstairs. I need to keep myself busy because I'm driving myself crazy with anticipation. I pour myself a finger of Moscatello and grab a biscotti from the jar in the bar I keep in my office.

I sit at my desk, turning on my laptop and forcing myself to look at spreadsheets. My clubs are doing well, even without the propped-up numbers from laundering my illegal funds. But my cash cow, as Americans would say, is my black-market import-export business. I move anything and everything from antiques, art, booze, and even regular commodities like olive oil.

When my father took over as Don, he not only had the mentorship of my grandfather, but he also had a formal education with degrees in business and accounting. My father told me there had once been a time when he thought he would make the Conte family legit, and in doing so he built businesses like the clubs that were very successful.

But there's something about crime that lures people in. Perhaps it's living on the edge. Maybe it's the cunning required to hide all your misdeeds in plain sight. Perhaps it's living in a world in which the laws are different and justice is delivered quickly.

My father passed down his teachings to me, and I run a well-oiled organization. Most of my men are the sons of the men who worked for my father, grandsons of the men who'd worked for my grandfather. If I have a problem, it doesn't come from within my organization. It comes from outside, either in the form of law enforcement trying to poke its head in my business or rival Families.

Today, it's Enzo Sabini who's causing me the most headache. The Contes and Sabinis have feuded for generations, but there had been a respect between the Dons. But Enzo is different. While his father operated similarly to my father, starting out with diplomacy and negotiations before reverting to violence, Enzo is an egomaniac hothead, drunk on power. I suppose that wouldn't be so bad if he wasn't such a fucking idiot.

For a while, Enzo was smart enough not to take me on directly, but over the last several months, he's been encroaching into my territories, occasionally causing disruption in the transport of my products. I recently gave him the respect he didn't deserve by meeting him face-to-face and giving him a warning. Apparently, he's decided not to heed it. In fact, I think by meeting with him, I boosted his ego, making him think he is more powerful than he really is. It won't be long before I have to kill him. Until that time, I have my men keeping an eye on Enzo and his men.

I look at my watch without even thinking, once again checking the time. Eleven. My plane leaves from New York in an hour. Will Aria be on it?

3

ARIA

What's that saying about doing the same thing over and over and expecting something different? If I decide not to get on the plane to Italy, I'm essentially signing up for the life that I currently have. A life I don't really like. So, with excitement and a whole lot of nerves, I rise from the edge of my bed and pull my bag out of the closet.

I've been vacillating for so long, I'm not sure that I've given myself enough time to get to the airport in White Plains. But I have to try.

I use my phone to order a rideshare to meet me a block away. God, I hope Niko isn't monitoring my phone in real time.

I peek out the hall and then make my way toward the back of the house, to the servants' staircase. There's no way I'll be able to make it out the front door without being seen. I just have to hope that none of the house staff is lingering.

I make it to the back stairs and head down, stopping before I reach the bottom landing. I listen to the left of me. Staff are in the kitchen preparing dinner. To the left are the servants' quarters. Their doors are shut.

I tiptoe as quickly as I can down the hall to the back door, pushing it open and stepping outside. This is where things get really tricky because there's no way into or out of Niko's property without a guard or alarm. Fortunately, I know there's a gate with a code, so my real challenge is the surveillance cameras. If I'm going to be stopped, it will likely be now.

I make my way through the garden, trying to stay close to the shrubs and trees until I reach the gate. I quickly poke in the number and hear the gate unlatch. I jerk it open and rush through, practically sprinting to the left toward the end of the block where the rideshare had better be waiting for me.

As I get closer to the corner, I look over my shoulder, expecting to see Danny or Marco or any of Niko's men coming after me. But I don't. I'm nearly free. The rideshare I ordered is a nondescript sedan that should blend in with every other car, and I'm relieved to see it's waiting. I open the back door, toss in my bag, and climb in.

"Aria?"

"Yes. Jacob, right?"

He hasn't yet pulled away from the curb, and I glance out the window, getting nervous. "I'm in a hurry."

"Hurry and driving through Manhattan aren't two words that go together, but I'll do my best." Finally, he pulls away into traffic. But I don't take a breath until we cross the bridge out of Manhattan.

As it gets closer and closer to six p.m., I'm nervous that I'm not going to make it. If that's the case, I have to keep my fingers crossed that I can sneak back into the house without anyone knowing I'd left.

Finally, the small private airport is visible.

"Here we are," Jacob the driver announces.

I grab my bag and open the door. "Thank you, Jacob." I figure I'll give him a good review and a large tip once I'm on the plane. I rush over to a hangar where a plane is being pulled out.

A man dressed in an expensive Italian suit looking like he stepped out of the pages of a men's fashion magazine is standing talking with a beautiful woman, also dressed immaculately.

As I approach, they both look up. The man tenses and steps slightly in front of the woman, and that's when I know I've come to the right place. He's ready to kill me if I'm here to cause trouble.

"I'm Aria Leone."

His gaze roams over me and his lips curve into a smirk. "I'm Bruno Castilla," he says in an Italian accent, thicker than Luca's. "And this is Simone Toscano."

He leans over to the woman and says something to her in Italian.

She nods and looks at me, waving a hand toward the plane. "*Venitev*," she says.

I know that. She's telling me to come.

Bruno holds his hand up toward the plane, and it stops. A moment later, the door opens and the stairs fold out.

"*Venitev in fretta*," she says. I think that means come quickly. I wonder if she speaks English. A moment of panic flares inside me that I'm going to a place where I don't speak or understand the language very well. I probably should've packed my English-Italian Dictionary.

But the worry dissipates as I think about learning Italian from Luca. I love to hear him speak his native language, even though I often don't understand what he's saying.

I hurry up the stairs, feeling equally eager to get going because I have no idea when Niko is going to notice that I'm gone. He could be on his way, using my phone to track me.

Simone guides me to a seat, and I sit, latching my belt. Bruno trots up the steps, his phone to his ear, speaking in Italian. When he hangs up, he speaks to the pilots, and then to Simone. Finally, he takes a seat across from me.

Once the plane is out of the hangar, it taxis to the runway. It feels like forever that we sit, and I keep looking out the window expecting Niko and his army to be driving in, guns blazing. But soon, I'm pressed back into the seat as the plane picks up speed down the runway. The nose lifts, and pretty soon, we're hovering over the ground, rising higher and higher toward the sky.

Bruno turns to the woman sitting near the cockpit. Lifting his finger, he says something to her in Italian, and the only word I recognize is *please*. Quickly, she gets up and goes to a small kitchen area on the plane, pulling out a bottle of champagne and a couple of flutes. Bruno laces his fingers across his middle as he studies me. I feel a little uncomfortable by it.

"It's not every day I am asked to kidnap a Mafia princess."

My hackles rise, and I sit up, pursing my lips at him. "I came willingly. It's hardly a kidnapping."

His lips twitch up. "I doubt your brother will see it like that."

He has a point.

"How long is the flight?" I ask, taking a flute of champagne from Simone.

"Little over eight hours. Plus, another hour or so to the villa. Signorina Leone, do you like the coast?

I nod, remembering Luca telling me about his villa and thinking it sounded like the most enchanted place on earth.

"You must be hungry. Simone, bring us our meal," Bruno orders.

"You speak good English. Do others at the villa?" I ask.

He smirks at me. "Don Conte's men speak English as a matter of doing business. But at the villa? Most who work there only have very basic English language they learned in school. I suspect you will be getting a crash course in Italian. It's a beautiful language, is it not? They say French is the language of love. But we all know it's Italian."

Even though we're on a small airplane whirling over the Atlantic Ocean, Simone serves us a traditional Italian dinner starting with fresh figs and salami. Next, she serves herbed chicken with vegetables, and of course, bread. We finish with an Italian ice and espresso, although I ask for decaf. I want to sleep on the plane. By my calculation, it will be two in the morning for me when we land in Rome, eight a.m. there. I want to be well rested when I see Luca.

I imagine first walking into Luca's villa, and a little sliver of nerves slides through me. But it's quickly quashed as I imagine him greeting me and embracing me, welcoming me to his home. I picture us continuing our long talks, maybe walking along the coast. I imagine him finally kissing me, and even taking me to his bed to claim me, and then waking up the next morning beside him.

By the time I drift to sleep on the plane, I'm eager to finally get to Luca and start living my happily ever after.

4

LUCA

"*Lei è sull'aereo e noi stiamo arrivando.*" Bruno's words offer me relief and excitement. Aria is on the plane and they're on their way. I imagine any moment, I'll be getting a call from Niko, but I have no concerns. Aria is coming to me of her own free will, and while Niko won't like it, there's very little he can do about it short of coming to Italy. If he does come, he won't get anywhere near her if he intends on dragging her back.

I check my watch again and do the time calculations. They will land in Rome around eight a.m. and arrive here close to ten.

I close down my computer and head upstairs to get some rest before Aria arrives. I drop my lounge pants and robe at the end of the bed, climbing in naked as I usually sleep. I'm generally a good sleeper, and I drift off easily.

My phone wakes me from a deep sleep. I look over at it expecting to see Niko's number, but I'm surprised to see Lucia's. I consider ignoring it, except that I like Lucia.

Her father in many ways was like Enzo Sabini, focused only on money and power at the expense of his daughters. Fortunately for

Lucia, or Lucy, as everyone seems to call her now, when my father bought her from her father, he was looking for a nursemaid and companionship, not a wife. She was very good to my father, and for that reason I'm in her debt, but only to a point. After all, I repaid the debt by allowing her to stay in the United States to be with Donovan Ricci and take over her father's business.

I pick up the phone. "*Pronto.*"

"Luca, do you know where Aria might be?"

I suppose technically, I do. She's somewhere over the Atlantic Ocean. "I am in Italy, Lucia." It's not a lie, but not an answer, either.

"Have you heard from her?"

"I have not spoken to Aria for nearly two weeks." That's true, too, isn't it? Sure, we passed notes, but we didn't speak in the normal sense of the word.

She's quiet on the other line, and I wait for what she might say next. Lucia is a kind woman, but she's not one to mince words and isn't afraid of me or anyone, as far as I know.

"What the hell, Luca?"

"What do you mean?"

"I know you're in love with her. The fact that you are not showing any concern about the fact that no one knows where she is tells me you know something."

Merda, I inwardly swear. Leave it to Lucia to be so astute. "You didn't say she was missing. You asked me where she was."

"Why in hell do you think I'd be calling you asking if you knew where she was if she wasn't missing?"

"Have you contacted your Bratva friends? I know Aria is quite fond of his wife or girlfriend or whatever she is."

"If find out you have something to do with this—"

"Careful of your next words, Lucia." I'm normally an easygoing, quiet sort of man, but I don't take threats well. "We are family. Do not make us enemies."

The line is silent for a moment. "If you do hear from her, tell her to call Niko. He's a fucking basket case that he can't find her."

"*Buona notte, Lucia.*" I press the button to end the call.

I don't like being in conflict with Lucia, but I must say there's satisfaction in knowing that Niko is losing his mind over his sister. I suppose that's mean because he could be imagining that she's dead. But it won't be long before that fear will be put to rest. Will he be grateful that she's only here with me? I doubt it.

I settle back in my pillow and into a deep sleep.

I'm awakened by my phone again. Cursing, I reach for the phone to discover it's 5:15 in the morning. Expecting Niko, I'm about to put the phone back down when I realize it's one of my men.

"*Pronto.*"

"We found what appears to be a bum skulking around the port. But Paolo recognizes him as one of Enzo's men. He's not speaking at the moment. We were going to kill him but were thinking you might want to talk to him. Maybe even just knowing you're on the way will make him talk."

I get out of bed. "Hold on. I'm on my way." By the time I arrive at the port, the sun is rising. I make my way to the office building of our legitimate shipping business and then down into the basement where the more unsavory acts happen.

There I find Paolo and Matteo talking together as they stand next to a man tied in a chair, passed out.

"Is this him?"

Both men straighten as I enter. "*Si.*"

"What's wrong with him?"

Paolo shrugs. "Sometimes, I don't know my own strength."

There are times when a line like that can be funny, but this isn't one of those times. I need to find out who this guy is and why he's skulking around my business. I poke at him, but he doesn't react.

I turn to my men. "What was he doing?"

"He was acting like a drunk and wandering around."

I study the man. He looks like a bum except that he doesn't smell bad or like alcohol, suggesting it's an act. "Did you check him for any sort of devices?"

"Yes."

"Any chance he's just a bum that's lost?"

"I'm pretty sure this is Antonio Cetta. He's one of Enzo's. Low level, but maybe he's trying to work his way up," Paolo explains.

"Paolo, stay here and watch him. Matteo, I want you to show me everywhere you think he was. I also want the surveillance pulled."

Matteo guides me along to where they had found our little friend. I scan the area looking for how he might have entered and what he might have seen.

Next we go to the office, and I review the surveillance video, noting that I couldn't see how he entered the area, which means there's a hole in the security, something I need to address right away.

"What are you doing here?" I ask rhetorically to the image on the screen.

Matteo and I return to the basement to find my intruder is awake. His eyes show the fear one might expect at seeing me, but he remains closed-lipped about his true purpose. He continues to tell me that he got lost, but now that he's sober, he'll be on his way.

"Interesting thing here, Antonio. I don't smell any alcohol on you. Surely, Enzo told you that to pull off a little stunt like this, you need to dab some liquor behind the ears, maybe pour a little bit on the front of your shirt. Perhaps go without a shower for a day or two. You smell way too fresh to be a drunkard bum."

His eyes flash with fear, and I wonder if it's of me or Enzo or both. Either way, this man is well and truly fucked. He decides to take his chance with me, staying loyal to Enzo by not revealing anything. I don't blame him. Enzo is a psychopath who will likely punish Antonio with torture, like ripping his fingernails out. Me? When a man needs to die, I find a shot to the head faster and easier.

I turn to Paolo and Matteo. "We need to check everything and get a sense of what he might have seen."

"If we kill him, he can't bring any information back to Enzo," Matteo says.

"But we don't know if he's already transmitted information to Enzo. Just because you didn't find anything on him doesn't mean he didn't dump it somewhere when he saw you two coming." Some might call me paranoid, but I like to think of it as careful and meticulous. I've already had one breach, so clearly, careful and meticulous are what I need to be, maybe even a little paranoid.

By the time I investigate all my offices, my shipping containers, and products, I don't have a sense that anything is missing or has been planted. That's some relief.

I check my watch and note that Aria landed nearly two hours ago. She'll be arriving at the villa any time, and I'm not there to greet her. That pisses me off.

"Load him up and take him to the prigione," I say of the medieval underground dungeon back at my estate.

Antonio's eyes widen. "*Piacere, Don Conte—*"

"So, you know who I am?" I turn to my men. "Load him up." I walk out fully expecting my men to comply.

We make the trip home, and as much as I want to run in and see Aria, I have to deal with my intruder. We drive to the side of the house, exiting our vehicles and escorting my new prisoner along the path that will take us down to one of the buildings where we house what we call the dungeon.

On the way, our prisoner keeps stopping to look around the grounds. It's an odd thing for him to be doing. This isn't a vacation.

The next time he turns to face the main house, I reach my hand out and grab him in the throat. "What the fuck are you doing?"

He shakes his head. "*Niente.*"

I don't buy that he's doing nothing. He's up to something. I look at Paolo and Matteo. "Are you sure you searched him for cameras or recording devices?"

"Absolutely."

I can't escape the idea that there is something on him recording what he's seeing. Perhaps he's live streaming back to Enzo. Technology today has gotten smaller, easier to conceal. I can imagine Enzo thinking of himself as some sort of *James Bond* spy.

I pull out my gun and hold it to the center of his forehead. "What the fuck are you doing?"

For the first time, the man shows real fear, dropping to his knees. "I am at your mercy, Don Conte."

I lower the gun to keep it pointed at his head. "Then tell me what you are doing."

He brings his hands together in a pleading gesture. "*Piacere, Don Conte.* Don't kill me. I have a family."

"No, you don't," Paolo says.

"I have a sick mother."

I roll my eyes at the cliché line, although I suppose it could be true. But I'm tired of this bullshit. I have a woman I've been pining after for months waiting for me.

I pull the trigger and watch as he crumples in a heap. "Wrap him in a tarp and take him into the dungeon. Search every millimeter of his body and his clothing. I want to know for sure that he hasn't transmitted any information about our business or my home to Enzo. Got it?"

My men look a little green around the gills, not so much because I killed this man but because they know it's possible they've messed up if Antonio was able to get information to Enzo.

I turn and stride back into the house, holstering my gun. I take the stairs up two by two and make a beeline toward the guest room. It's time for me to make Aria Leone mine.

5

ARIA

When I arrived at Luca's villa, I was disappointed to learn that he wasn't there, that he had been called away at the last minute on business.

But his housekeeper, Roberta, who spoke very little English, showed me up to a lovely room that made me think of a medieval castle. I explored the room, and now I sit in the plush chaise lounge chair next to a window that overlooks the large grounds and beyond to the sea. I did it. I'm here.

I imagine by now, Niko has noticed that I've gone. He's probably tried to call, but once we landed in Rome, Bruno took my phone, telling me I would be given a new one.

I'm not sure whether they don't want me to have my old phone because it's on an American cellular plan or to make it harder for Niko to contact me. A tinge of guilt settles in my stomach for having left the way I did, and I suspect that Niko is worried.

But he has Luca's number if he figures out that I'm here, and I imagine Luca will allow me to contact him to let him know that I'm safe.

With nothing else to do and accepting the idea that this will be my home, at least for a little while, I rise from the comfy chair to unpack my bag. As I put my clothes in the dresser and closet, I can see they are already filled with clothes.

At first, jealousy flares, imagining that this must be one of Luca's girl-friends' rooms, but then I notice the tags are still on the items. I smile because there's something sweet about the idea of Luca arranging for me to have clothes to wear when I got here.

I put my toiletries in the bathroom and gasp at the size of the large standalone tub. I'm tempted to fill it and take a soak in it, but I want to be able to meet Luca when he arrives home, so a luxurious soak will have to wait.

I hear movement outside the door. It's the type of sound that happens in Niko's house when he's arriving back home after being away for a bit.

I go to the door, stepping into the hall. I make my way down the stairs where servants are bustling about. I see Roberta and wave her over. In my broken Italian, I ask her if Luca is arriving home.

"*Si.*" She guides me to a room off the back of the house. It has gorgeous floor-to-ceiling windows overlooking his estate and the ocean beyond. She says something in Italian but uses her hands, pumping in a downward motion that I take to mean that I can wait there.

"*Grazie.*"

When she leaves, I go to the large windows, noting there is a door to the outside terrace. I picture being in this room with Luca, talking and enjoying the view on cold, stormy nights, but sitting out on the lovely terrace on days like today.

A movement off to the left catches my attention. I see Luca with three men. Two of them appear to work for him, and the third looks like a poor homeless man. They walk toward another building on the property. I wonder what's going on.

The homeless man keeps looking around, often turning and gazing up toward the house. Finally, Luca stops him. I can't see Luca's face, but whoever this man is, he's definitely in the wrong place at the wrong time.

All of a sudden, Luca whips out his gun and presses the barrel to the man's forehead. I gasp, bringing my hands to my lips to keep from crying out.

What is he doing? He's not going to kill the man simply for wandering onto his land, is he? The poor guy looks like he needs food, a bath, and to be taken to a homeless shelter.

The man drops to his knees, bringing his hands together in a pleading motion. My heart goes out to him. He must realize who he's dealing with. Luca is probably just scaring some sense into him so that once he sets the man free, he won't return.

A loud bang sounds, reverberating all the way to me and into my chest. The man crumples to the ground.

"My God." I recoil as Luca turns and makes his way toward the house. I know it is Luca, and yet he doesn't look like the man I know. His expression is fierce, his eyes are dark, almost dead looking. As he moves closer, he runs his fingers through his dark hair, and his expression morphs, softens into the Luca I know. It's like he's removed one mask and put on the one I recognize. But I cannot unsee what I just saw. Luca is cruel and merciless.

I rush out of the room toward the stairs. Roberta intercepts me. She must see that I'm upset. She cocks her head and speaks to me in Italian, but I have no clue what she's saying.

"He just killed somebody." I make a motion with my thumb and forefinger like a gun, bringing it to my head.

She seems to understand what I'm saying, but the confusion in her expression suggests she doesn't know why I am upset. I push away from her and make my way up the stairs into my room, shutting and locking the door.

I find my bag in the closet and began packing the clothes I'd only just unpacked minutes ago. Fortunately, I don't have that much, and everything is back in my bag within minutes. The next task is figuring out how I get out of here. I doubt I can simply walk out. Luca's villa sits in the rural countryside, not in the middle of a large city like Niko's does. Once I got out of here, where would I go and how would I get there?

A knock on the door startles me.

"Aria? It's Luca. Open the door so I can properly welcome you to my home."

I swallow and glance around the room, seeking an escape. "No."

"Is there something wrong, *Mio Angelo*? Open the door and tell me what the problem is."

I don't say anything. Instead, I go to the window, wondering if I can get out that way. It's on the second floor, and I'm still stuck with not knowing how I would get off the property and to a place where I could get help. Then again, who would help? I imagine that Luca is known by everyone in the region, and no one would dare cross him.

Luca starts speaking Italian, and I get the sense he's speaking to someone else. A woman I recognize as Roberta responds.

"Fuck," comes Luca's response.

I learned long ago in my travels through Europe that the F word is universal.

"Aria. You will open the door. I will not be locked out of a room in my own house."

I can't say that his tone is angry, but it's definitely firm. It is a command.

"I made a mistake. I want to go home," I say.

There's a pause for a moment. "To do that, you'll have to open the door. Please don't make me open it for you."

I close my eyes, knowing I'd be an idiot to go against him. I hear Roberta speaking, and the knob jostles, and then the door pops open.

Luca says something to her in Italian, and she nods, scurrying away. He enters the room, and I rush around to the other side of the bed as if it's a barrier that will protect me.

For long moments, he stares at me. "What is the problem, Aria?"

"You killed that poor homeless man. Why did you do that? He's innocent."

Luca lets out a derisive laugh. "That man is not homeless or innocent. He works for an enemy of mine. Should I have allowed him to live so that he could come slit my throat in the middle of the night? Or worse, yours?"

"Did you have to kill him?"

He sets his hands on his hips and tilts his head to the side, looking at me in confusion. "You are the child of a Mafia Don. The sister of a Mafia Don. Surely, you know what happens in our world."

Of course I know about the life my brother leads, but this is different. "I've never seen my brother kill anybody." The only time I've witnessed someone kill was when Lucy shot Lou who at the time was planning to kill her, Elena, and me. That was self-defense. Luca killed a man who was on his knees begging for his life.

His expression softens. "I am sorry that I had to be the one to expose you to the darker side of Mafia life." He takes a step toward me, but I recoil.

"What is it, Aria?"

"You... you are a monster."

He flinches and doesn't seem to like what I've called him. But he gives me a smile. "Sometimes, my work requires such brutality, just as for your brother. But look at me now, *Mio Angelo*. Don't you see the man who has waited so long to make you his?"

Roberta returns to the room carrying a tray with a bottle of champagne and two flutes. She sets them on a table near the window and then leaves.

Luca goes to the table and opens the bottle, pouring the bubbly into the glasses.

"I don't want champagne," I say.

He smiles as he holds a glass to me. "It's *Franciacorta*, Italian champagne. Take the glass and we can talk."

I recall that only sparkling wine from the Champagne region of France can be called champagne. Not that it matters now.

Deciding I'm better off to go along and hope he'll arrange to send me home, I take the flute.

"To *Mio Angelo*. I'm so happy to have you here." He clicks his glass against mine. He sips, watching me over the rim of his glass. I give in, taking a sip. This moment should be happy, even giddy. All I feel is stupidity for thinking I'd be walking into a fairy tale.

Luca steps away, sitting in the window seat. "So, tell me about your big escape and your grand adventure to get here."

I look down into my glass. "I think it was a mistake."

"Tell me anyway."

I sit on the edge of the bed knowing I'm trapped. I explain how I snuck out of the house and through the garden. He laughs in delight, and there's a lightness about it that I remember from our stolen moments over the last few months. I'm with the man I remember, but I can't get the image of the callous, vicious man I just saw.

"I knew you'd get away. You're very clever, resourceful. Adventurous."

I shrug thinking about the statement, *Be careful what you wish for.*

"How was the flight? Bruno treated you well, did he not?"

I nod.

"I wish I could have been there, but if Niko knew I was in town, he'd keep a closer eye on you."

I sigh and nod again.

"Thank you for your notes."

I look up at him. How could the man who came up with the ingenious, ultra-romantic way to communicate so emotionlessly kill that poor man?

"I still have them." He shakes his head and laughs. "They smell like you. I'm like a lovesick schoolboy."

My heart squeezes, and I realize his words are seeping in, softening me to him. Maybe I'm overreacting. I mean, it's not like I don't know who is... what he is. Although I've never seen my brother kill someone who was begging for mercy, I have seen the same lethal expression on him, usually at times he was concerned about me or Elena.

"Why did you kill that man?"

I see a flicker of annoyance in his eyes, but he answers. "He was spying on my business. I brought him here to question him. Normally, I might not have done that, but I was eager to get home and see you. His behavior... the way he was looking around... I didn't like it." He stands and slowly comes toward me.

I tense but don't move to avoid him.

"I'm surprised at your reaction. Your brother is *Il Soldato della Morte*. Surely, you understand how this all works."

"It's one thing to know it, another to see it. The only time I ever saw someone killed was when Lucy shot a man trying to kill us."

Luca smiles. "I always knew Lucia was a fierce woman. I always knew that if someone came after my father in his time of weakness, she'd dispatch them without a thought. I'm so glad she was there to save you, *Mio Angelo*." He sits next to me. "You've been sheltered, protected. Don't you see, that's what I'm doing too?"

I close my eyes as warring emotions, one of desire and the other fear, vie for attention. Can I trust this man?

"I have wanted you for a long time, Aria. You're mine now. Mine to claim. Mine to protect. Mine to spoil."

"What if I want to leave?"

"You have proven you want me by running away from your brother and risking his wrath to be with me."

I look at him even though I know by doing so, any strength I might have to keep him at bay will be lost. "That was before."

He takes my hand. "Would you stop caring for your brother if you saw him kill an intruder? Why is my protecting what's mine... protecting you... any different from what Lucia did?"

"Lou didn't beg for his life."

"Did he have a chance to?"

No, but... everything when Lucy killed Lou happened so fast. Even so, Luca's words are making sense. Or maybe it's that I just want them to make sense.

He leans in closer, his warmth and scent swirling around me, making me dizzy with yearning. "I missed you." His lips press against my cheek, and my resolve slips even further away.

"I've thought of nothing but this moment for so long." His lips trail along my jaw and down my neck. "Tell me you feel the same."

The words, 'No, I don't feel the same,' dissipate like smoke from my mind. "Luca."

"*Si, Mio Angelo?*" His lips continue to caress and kiss. It's intoxicating, and I can't respond.

His hand cups my cheek and turns my head to look at him. "You're mine now."

There's no fighting it. I nod, and the next moment, his lips are on mine, his kiss an all-consuming inferno I feel in every cell of my body.

"There's my woman." He pushes me back on the bed. Or maybe I lie back and pull him with me. I'm not sure. All I know is that all of a sudden, my body is hot and needy for his touch.

His lips are everywhere along my skin, and only when he kisses me on the mouth again do I realize I'm naked. I growl in frustration that he's still dressed and tug at his clothes.

"There's no rush, *Mio Angelo*." He stops my hands, and once again, his lips trail over my body and down. "Such a beautiful body," he murmurs.

"Luca." I pull at him, needing him now.

"You need satisfaction?"

"You... I need you."

"Words to my ears, *tesoro mio*." My treasure. He's a romance novel Alpha male come to life. He moves down my body, his tongue lapping over my breasts. The sensation shoots down between my thighs, and I moan in frustration. He sucks my nipples until I'm whimpering with need.

"Let me make you feel good." He moves lower and lower, pushing my legs apart.

"Luca." I reach for him again, needing him, but then his tongue slides through my folds and holy moly, I nearly come out of my skin. It feels so good. "Oh, God." My hand holds his head to me, wanting more.

He licks and sucks, and my body isn't my own as it rocks and pulses to his touch. Need coils tighter and tighter until I'm about to come apart. It's both torturous and magnificent all at once.

His tongue slides inside me as his thumb brushes over my clit, and oh... my... God. My body explodes. It shatters into a billion pieces, sending me flying. The pleasure is amazing. The sensation hovers and then begins to dissipate until he inserts a finger, then two, inside me, and all of a sudden, I'm at the edge again.

"Luca... Oh, God..." I arch, my body tense as it detonates again.

"So delicious," he murmurs as his tongue laps at me. He moves up my body, kissing me. I can taste myself, which should feel icky but doesn't.

He takes my hand, guiding it to his dick. I gasp at how thick and hard it is. Even after two explosive orgasms, my pussy clenches in anticipation.

I stroke him and he groans. "It's time, *piccola*." He settles over me, his hips insinuating between my legs. He holds himself over me on his forearms as he gazes down at me.

"Did you just call me little?"

His smile is sweet. "It's a term of endearment. I believe in America, you say *baby*. It's time, baby." His dick brushes against me, and I arch as wave of need rushes through me. I grip his hips and open for him.

He kisses me. "You cannot change your mind after this. Do you understand? You'll be mine."

I nod, but it's the desperate need for him that is responding. Whatever I need to agree to, I will if it means he'll make me his.

He thrusts, and a shockwave of sensation blasts through me. It starts with a pinch of pain and moves to a feeling of fullness. And then it pulses with an amazing building pressure of pleasure.

He lets out a stream of Italian words that I don't know the meaning of. He begins to pull away, but I wrap my legs around him.

"More... *più*..." I use the Italian word, although I'm not sure I'm using it right.

"Aria..." His voice is tight.

I rock my hips, and he releases more Italian words as he levers up on his hands. He moves in and out, and the friction is beyond anything I've ever felt. Of course it is, as I've never been with a man like this before. I'm not a prude, but I am a romantic, and so I saved myself for the man I love. For Luca.

6

LUCA

This is not good. Well, that's not true. Being inside Aria's hot, wet pussy is the closest thing to heaven I'll ever reach.

But if I'm not mistaken, the tightness from that first thrust, the way she gasped and winced, tells me I'm the first man to be inside her delectable body. I didn't even consider that she might be a virgin.

Yes, in many ways, she's been sheltered, but she's an outgoing, lively woman who's traveled the world. I assumed that sex was one of the experiences she would've had by now.

My next thought brings feelings of guilt. I shouldn't have just driven into her like I did. I should have taken more time, given her more care. In fact, considering she waited this long, saved herself, I should have married her first.

I next grapple with the fact that taking her virginity will give Niko an even stronger reason to see me dead. I can't see where marrying her after-the-fact will change his attitude toward me. My only saving grace is that I asked for her hand beforehand, so perhaps I can put the blame back on him.

Aria arches, her legs wrapping around my hips, pulling me tighter, and that sweet pussy of hers sends sensations that push away all my concerns.

"More... *più*..."

"Aria..." I'm on the verge of losing it.

She rocks her hips, and a stream of vulgar words escapes my lips. They're in Italian, so I don't think she understands. I lever up on my hands and drive inside her. It feels so fucking good the way her pussy squeezes around me, draws me in. I'm no stranger to fucking, but I'm certain my dick has never been fucked like this.

I thrust in again, watching her as I do. Her tits bounce, her head tilts back, and she lets out a moan that makes my dick thicken, harden. The only thing that keeps me from losing control is the desire to watch her come.

If I'm right, this will be her first orgasm by dick.

I want it to be spectacular for her.

I want her to remember it for the rest of her days. Whatever happens to us in the future, I want this moment seared into her brain. If something goes awry and we're not together, I want me and this moment to ruin any other men for her.

The idea of another man being with her like this, now that I'm fairly certain I'm the first, is untenable. She's mine, has always been mine from the moment I met her. And right now, I'm claiming her. Not Niko, not anyone can take her from me.

"Oh, God... Luca... oh, oh, oh!"

She's so beautiful as the pressure builds. She's responsive. With each thrust, her pussy clenches and she arches.

"Come, *Mio Angelo*... let me see you come." I'm picking up the pace, losing the battle of control as my cock sizzles with electric fire. I shift, thrust, and grind against her pussy.

"Yes... Luca..."

I do it again, and she cries out, her body going taut, her pussy clamping down around my cock until I see stars. Power surges through me until I'm unable to hold back. I piston in and out of her, the pressure coiling tight until I drive in and my world explodes.

"Fuck!" I yell out as my release barrels through me like a freight train.

"Oh, my God!" Aria cries out again, her pussy gripping me hard in another orgasm.

I drive in and out, in and out, drawing out the pleasure until my arms give out and I collapse over her.

Even as I struggle to catch my breath, her pussy pulses and my cock throbs. I manage to roll off her but pull her in next to me. She nestles into my side, her head on my shoulder. I wonder if I need to ask her about her virginity. But what would it matter? She's mine now.

My cum is inside her as proof. For a moment, I consider that I didn't consider birth control, but again, what does it matter? She's mine.

Her breathing slows and her body goes pliant. I look down and realize she's sleeping. I remind myself that she's traveled a long way and is suffering from jetlag. I need to let her rest, and I have work to do.

I extricate myself from her side and quietly dress. I exit the bedroom and make my way downstairs, finding Roberta to tell her that once Aria awakens, she's to move all of Aria's belongings into my room. Since Aria has proven that she wants to be with me, there's no sense in her staying in another room.

I head out of the house to visit the dungeon, taking in the fresh, sweet air between my home and the outbuilding. The scent in the air is sweeter, the sun warmer. That's Aria's doing, but I can't allow my flights of fancy to interfere with business. As I enter the building and make my way down to the dark, damp place that has held prisoners for hundreds of years, I put on my game face.

When I enter where Paolo and Marco have taken Enzo's lackey, I find the man stripped bare and his clothes practically in tatters. My men look up at me with concern in their expressions, telling me that this man had something compromising on him. I'd learned long ago there is no sense asking questions you already know the answer to, unless of course you want to find out whether someone is lying to you.

Knowing there is something, I demand, "What was it? Where was it?"

"It was sewn into his jacket, hiding in the zipper."

That would make it very small. What could it possibly record? "Audio? Video?"

"Camera and audio," Paolo says.

Mother fucker. "I need you to go back to the docks and take another look at what he might have sent to Sabini. And I want extra men, got it?"

My men shake their heads, and the terror in her eyes tells me that they'll do what they're told. They know they're on shaking ground and need to make this up to me.

I nod toward the body, for a moment feeling bad for the man who allowed himself to be taken in by Enzo Sabini. I consider dumping the poor dumb slob on Sabini's doorstep but decide that making this man disappear will unnerve him more.

Uncertainty can be unsettling. Sabini will likely figure out I took his man, but with no evidence of this man ever existing, he'll know I have the power and influence to make him disappear as well. Perhaps he'll think twice about fucking with me again.

"Cremate him. Spread his ashes in the vineyard. Get Toscano to purge all his papers." I mention one of the many men I have on my payroll who work in government and law enforcement. "I want all evidence of this man's existence destroyed." I think of Aria and how upset she was that I'd killed a man she felt was innocent. Would she find my actions now unpalatable? I shake away the thought. I can't let what she thinks impact my decisions.

My men nod, and I exit the dungeon, heading back to my home office. Just as I sit at my desk, the phone rings. My lips curve up as I recognize the number from the United States.

I poke the answer button. "*Pronto.*"

The line is quiet for several long moments, but I don't say anything. The silence tells me that Niko is pissed, and while I could hang up, I wait to hear what he has to say. I figure I'll let him speak his mind because this will be the last time we talk.

"Who the fuck do you think you're messing with?"

"Is there a problem?" I ask, my tone dismissive.

"Don't play coy with me, you motherfucker. I know you kidnapped my sister—"

"I did no such thing. In fact, I warned you that at some point, Aria would take control of her life. I even went to you, out of respect, to do this right, but you—"

"And I told you no."

"And what did Aria tell you? I doubt you even asked her, did you? Do you really care about your sister's happiness?" I sit back in my chair, enjoying Niko's tirade. I respect him as a businessman. He's smart and ruthless, but he lacks respect for traditions set forth by my ancestors. It's probably why the American Mafia is dying.

"She is my responsibility—"

"Not anymore." I'm forced to consider that while Aria came to me, she does love her brother. Perhaps it isn't wise for me to cut her off from him entirely. I know enough about human behavior to know that could backfire. Sure, I can keep her against her will, but that's not what I want. "She's here and safe and where she wants to be. My goal is for her to be happy, and to that end, I'm sure there is some sort of agreement that you and I can come to, assuming you care about her happiness as well."

"You're a dead man, Luca Conte."

I sigh. "I suppose time will tell. And here's my threat to you, Niko. You so much as set foot into Italy, and I assure you that you will never return home. What a shame it would be for your beautiful wife and children to live the rest of their days without you." I don't wait for a response, clicking the line off and dropping the phone to my desk.

I scrape my hands over my face because the truth is that I don't want to make an enemy of Niko.

When I think of the business we can do together, I see a fortune and power for the both of us. Unfortunately for him, he's willing to let his ego not only ruin what could be a lucrative relationship, but a close one with his sister as well.

I push Niko out of my mind and focus on the job at hand. For the next few hours, I shore up all my business properties to protect them from whatever Enzo is planning. But my method is subtle. I want to catch him in the act. Like a moth to a flame, I plan to lure him in and finally get rid of him.

It's late afternoon when I head back to the kitchen where I find my cook and Roberta working.

"In America they eat dinner earlier than us, don't they?" I ask.

Both ladies look at each other and shrug. I normally have my dinner between eight and nine, but when I was in America, they ate closer to six or seven.

"I want a full Italian meal served at seven. Pull out all the stops. I want a celebration for my guest."

They both bow their heads to me and say, "*Si, Don Conte.*"

"Have you moved her into my room yet?" I ask Roberta.

Roberta gives a single shake of her head. "I did not want to disturb her. But as soon as she wakes, we are prepared to make the move."

"Good."

I exit the kitchen and go to my library, pouring myself two fingers of Scotch whiskey and carry it out onto the terrace. I breathe in, and as I exhale, I feel strangely content. It's not a feeling I'm used to.

My father's words come back to me. He was on his deathbed, and I was eager to contact Lucia in New York to bring her home because she had been the one thing keeping him alive. But he shook his head, saying it was time for Lucia to have her own life, that he owed her for all that she had given him.

Before he closed his eyes and took his last breath, he told me, "The secret to power in our life, my son, is in the wife you choose to be your other half. Beauty and the body are nice, yes, but a woman's love and devotion to you, along with intelligence, is the true secret to a man's success. You are prepared to take over the business, Luca, but it's time that you stop fucking around and find the woman who will be the source of your power."

At the time, I thought it was the nice ramblings of a dying man. It wasn't until the first time I saw Aria at Niko's penthouse that my father's words made sense. The draw to her was immediate, as if she were my other half.

And now she's here. Her presence makes me feel powerful beyond belief. Invincible. And nothing, not Niko, not Enzo, will take her away from me.

7

ARIA

As consciousness approaches, I feel disoriented. Where am I?

I open my eyes, and it takes a second, but then I realize I'm at Luca's villa. The giddiness fills me as I lie back in bed and grin up at the ceiling. I inhale, and I can still smell him on the sheets surrounding me. Fairytales do come true.

The door pops open, and I sit up, letting the sheet fall, thinking it's Luca back to touch me again. My nipples harden in anticipation, and I work to pose seductively.

Roberta enters the room and stands next to the bed. Embarrassed, I hold the sheet up to cover myself. If she has any thoughts about my appearance, it doesn't register on her face. It makes me wonder how many times she's found other women in a similar state of undress.

"Shower?" She makes a motion of washing. She follows up with a sentence in Italian in which the only thing I recognize is the word for dinner. Through deduction, I determine I'm supposed to shower for dinner.

I nod but am reluctant to get out of bed completely naked. Roberta goes to the closet, takes out a robe, and brings it over, holding it up for me. I decide that this is something she's probably used to.

It makes me think back to the castles I've visited in Europe in which I learned that much of the king's daily routine included sitting on the pot while his staff went through his day with him and then helped him dress. I'm not going to go as far as to have Roberta watch me go potty or wipe my butt, but I think I can manage getting out of bed naked and have her help me put on a robe.

I take my time in the shower, making sure the pretty scented soap is leathered all over my body. I wash my hair, knowing it will take extra time to dry it but wanting to look perfect for my first official dinner in Luca's home.

When I exit the shower, I put the robe back on and set about cleansing my face so I can put on new makeup. I pull the towel from my head, brushing out my hair. I find a blow dryer and dry my hair until it's only slightly damp. I put in mousse, scrunching my hair all over to get nice, soft, natural waves.

I leave the bathroom and find a beautiful emerald dress lying on the bed. Next to it are a matching pair of bra and panties and a pair of black stiletto heels. An erotic chill slides through me at the idea of Luca removing them from my body later tonight. I put on the garments and the dress, then look at myself in the mirror. I look good. I hope Luca agrees.

A few moments later, Roberta enters, taking a long look at me and giving a nod of approval.

"*Ti sta aspettando,*" she says. I'm pretty sure that means that Luca is waiting for me.

I slip on the heels and follow her out of my room and down the stairs. She guides me to an area of the house that I'd only glanced at earlier.

She opens the double doors. The room is lit with candles on the table, and soft music plays.

Across the room, Luca is standing, his back to me as he looks out the window. As I enter, he turns and my breath stalls in my lungs. He is dressed in a dark suit, and his hair is slicked back. He looks powerful and sexy. Like an Italian James Bond.

He smiles as he walks toward me. "You are beautiful, *Mio Angelo*." He puts his hands on my arms and leans in, kissing me on one cheek, and then the other. "Are you hungry?"

Hunger is an understatement. "I'm famished."

He smiles and guides me toward the table, holding my chair out as I sit. He says something to Roberta in Italian that I think means we're ready to eat.

He sits at the head of the table, and for a moment, I feel like a queen. I grew up in elegance and luxury, but there's something different about it in a home built hundreds of years ago and chock-full of history. Here it feels like royalty, not just riches.

A few moments later, a servant arrives with the aperitivo of prosecco and nuts. Luca holds up his glass. "Welcome home, Aria."

I have dueling emotions from his words, excitement and at the same time, fear. Is this really going to be my home?

Until now, this has been a big adventure, but I realize that my decision has set a new course for my life. I remind myself that this is what I want. I click my glass with his.

"Are you well?" he asks.

"Yes." I worry that his question is leading to asking about our encounter this afternoon. Is he going to ask me about being a virgin?

"So, you're settling in?"

I nod with relief that I don't have to talk about my virginity. Maybe he didn't notice.

As each course of the meal comes, our conversation becomes easier and easier, like it had been on our outings in New York. We talk about anything and everything, although nothing of real consequence except to learn a little bit about each other. His favorite color is green, which is why I suspect I'm wearing an emerald dress.

Having napped for so long, I worry about being able to sleep tonight, but as the eighth and last course of the meal, the *digestivo* of limoncello arrives, I'm feeling full and lethargic.

Luca rises from his chair, coming to stand next to me, holding out his hand. "Come with me. I have a surprise."

I grin and probably look like a silly schoolgirl. "I don't need surprises."

He smiles as he leans forward and kisses me on the cheek. "But I like giving them to you all the same." He loops my arm through his, escorting me out of the dining room and to the stairs. When we reach the landing, instead of heading in the direction of my room, we go across the hall and enter an expansive suite. I thought my room was rich and decadent, but this room is definitely fit for a king.

"This is your room now, Aria." His eyes stare at me intently, as if he's wanting me to understand this is a statement, not a question. I don't have a choice, not that I want one.

Sure, the feminist in me feels he should ask me if I want to share a room with him. But the woman in me is all gooey inside at the idea of going to bed and waking up in the morning next to this man. It's crazy considering how little I really know him.

Even the memory of his brutality toward that strange man this afternoon can't take away the feeling that I've just entered a dream.

I give him my best flirty smile. "Is it time for bed?"

He laughs, and it's free and beautiful. "In due time, *Mio Angelo*. First..." He takes my hand and guides me to an ensuite bathroom that is almost as large as my entire bedroom back at Niko's.

An enormous tub sits surrounded by a bay window through which moonlight shimmers. Luca turns on the water and pours oils into it. As the tub fills, he comes over to me, his eyes capturing mine as he unzips my dress and slowly peels it off my shoulders until it falls away and pools around my ankles.

I shiver from the light touch of his knuckles as he brushes them down my arms and then around to my back to unclasp my bra. It falls away, and his eyes immediately go to my breasts. Hunger fills them, but he only brushes the tips with his thumbs and then he tugs down my panties.

"It's your turn now," I say, wanting to see him naked again.

He shakes his head as he guides me to the tub. "This is for you." He helps me in, and I settle into the warm, fragrant water.

"I'll be right back." He's not gone long when he re-enters with two flutes of more Prosecco, handing me one. I keep thinking he's going to join me, but he doesn't.

We clink our glasses again and then he sets his aside. He kneels by the tub, taking a soft cloth that he runs through the water and then caresses it over my shoulders and arms.

He's behind me now as he leans in and gives me a kiss at the nape of my neck. "Did I hurt you today?"

I tense, wondering if he's talking about the sex.

"No."

The washcloth brushes along my shoulders and back. "I think it was your first time, was it not?"

I close my eyes in embarrassment. "What does it matter?"

"It matters because that is a precious gift. I don't know if I'm worthy of it."

I turn my head to look back at him. "I wouldn't have given it if I didn't find you worthy."

His smile is soft, sweet as he leans down and presses another kiss to the nape of my neck. I don't think it's meant to be arousing, but I feel it in my entire body. My nipples harden. My pussy pulses with need.

"I would have been gentler had I known. But this bath should help with any soreness."

"I don't mind the soreness." Truth be told, I kind of like it. Not that I like pain, but it's a badge of honor. I'd had sex, and I'd had it with the man I'd chosen. "When do we get to do it again?"

His lips are on my skin again as he chuckles. "I wish it could be tonight, but alas, you need your rest."

I try not to pout. "I feel fine. I had a long nap, and you gave me an espresso." That was the caffe course before the *digestivo*.

"It was decaf, although don't tell anybody. It might ruin my reputation as an Italian."

I take his hand and pull him so that he's beside me. "I really want to do it again."

"My poor aroused little angel." He leans in and kisses me. This time, it's not the sweet little kisses but a powerful, fierce, arousing one. I'm trying to pull him in the tub with me, but he's big and resists.

"Relax. Let me take care of you." His hand slides down my body and between my thighs.

I start to tell him that I want him naked, but his fingers slide against my clit and I gasp at the pleasure that shoots through me.

"Close your eyes," he says softly, his lips brushing along my shoulder as his fingers work wonders.

"What about you?" I ask breathlessly.

"All I need is to see your pleasure. It feels nice, yes?"

"Yes." I close my eyes and give in to his touch. I might have been a virgin, but I wasn't new to orgasms. I'd touched myself plenty of times. Somehow, his touching me isn't like that. It's better, and soon, my hips are rocking and I'm gasping for breath as I teeter on the edge of a cliff.

"Pinch your nipples." His voice is rough, edgy. It tells me this is turning him on.

I do as he commands, my fingers squeezing my hard nipples. "Oh!" I feel the pinch straight to my center, and before I know it, water is sloshing about as I come hard around Luca's fingers.

As I come down, I feel boneless in the warm water. Luca continues to wash me and trail kisses over my skin. It's the most romantic moment of my life, and all my doubts about what I've done wash away.

When I'm finished, he helps me out of the tub, putting a robe on me. "Come to bed."

I shake my head. "I want a turn." My hand covers his groin where his erection is evident.

"This isn't about me."

"No. It's about me wanting to make you come." I undo his belt. I see uncertainty in his eyes. He wants me to take care of him, but he's not sure he wants to deviate from his plan. "Don't you want me to be happy?"

"I live for it, *Mio Angelo*."

"Then let me do this." I push his pants down, his dick bouncing loose. It's long and hard, and I'm fascinated by it. But I'm also inexperienced, and so for a moment, doubt has me rethinking this.

His finger tilts my chin up. "You don't have to—"

"I want to." I sink to my knees. I look up at him, and something in his eyes flashes with wild heat.

"Your innocence makes me hungry for you," he growls out.

"Tell me what you like."

He takes his dick in hand and rubs the tip along my lips. "Simply suck it. Like a… *il leccalecca…*" He frowns. "A candy on a stick."

"Lollipop?"

He nods. "Yes. Lollipop."

It's been a while since I had a lollipop, but I feel confident I remember how to consume one. I lick the tip, tasting a sweet, salty drop of precum.

He growls as I lick around the rim. Finally, I suck the tip into my mouth, swirling the velvety tip with my tongue.

"*Si, Mio Angelo.*" He closes his eyes, and his hips rock gently as I suck him deeper. He speaks in Italian, mostly words I don't know, but I get the feeling they're dirty. It makes me feel sexy and powerful.

His fingers lace through my hair, holding my head as his movements pick up speed, his thrusts go deeper. I'm a little worried if he goes too deep, so I wrap my hand around his dick, using it and my mouth to stroke him.

"Ah… *basta…* enough… stop…"

I do as he asks and look up at him, wondering what I'm doing wrong.

"I'm going to come," he says gently.

"That's the point, right?" I'm not seeing the problem.

"Some women don't like it."

"I don't know if I like it until I try it."

Again, fire flashes in his eyes. Like he's excited by the idea of coming in my mouth. It turns me on that he's turned on. I bring his dick to my mouth and suck it hard and deep.

He lets out a string of Italian again. His dick is so hard, I can feel the ridges, feel it pulsing. I focus on tightening around him with my lips.

"Si... Aria... ah..." He lets out a long, feral growl and thrusts until I nearly gag. Warm liquid coats my tongue, fills my mouth as he continues to rock in and out of my mouth.

A moment later, he hauls me up by my arms and kisses me hard. He must taste himself in the kiss, and that's erotic too. He moves me to the counter, lifting me until I sit on it. Then he's on his knees and his mouth is on me. I'm already so hot, so needy, that immediately, I'm gasping, and my pussy is on fire.

"Luca... oh, God..."

His tongue does the most marvelous things. Flicking over my clit. Sliding in my pussy. It's not long before pleasure explodes through me. It rockets through me until I'm boneless again.

Luca rises, kisses me tenderly. He picks me up and carries me to his bed. Now our bed.

"Sleep well, *Mio Angelo*," he says as he tucks me in.

"You're not joining me?"

He gives me an apologetic expression. "I have work."

"What's the point of my being in your room if you're not here too?"

He smiles. "You're very right." He lies next to me, spooning around me. I know he'll be up once I'm asleep. I don't love that, but I know I have time to change that. Someday, we'll be going to bed and rising together in the morning. Maybe we'll have kids. Maybe, when we're really old, we'll die in each other's arms. Yes, fairy tales do come true.

8

ARIA

I wake in a dim room. It takes me a moment to reorient myself. I'm in Luca's bedroom in Italy. Turning toward the other side of the bed, I see that it's empty. I'm disappointed but not surprised. I recall that when he put me to bed last night, Luca had indicated that he had more work to do.

It occurs to me that in the twenty-four hours I've been here, Luca has been gone more than present. He wasn't here when I arrived, even though he knew I was coming. He was the one who arranged my trip.

An uneasy feeling settles inside me. How does Luca see our relationship? When I'd see him in New York, his focus was one hundred percent on me when we were together.

But now that I'm here, he isn't around. Not when I arrived, and not now, first thing in the morning. I'm not even sure he joined me in the middle of the night. Here I've had fantasies of a fairytale life, but maybe I'm just some dalliance to him.

I try to shake away my insecurities. I think back to the notes we'd passed in New York. It took a lot of planning and effort for him to arrange that. Then he'd arranged for me to come to Italy. Surely, that's a sign that I'm more than just a fling to him.

A knock on the door draws my attention away from my thoughts. The door pops open and Roberta steps in.

"*Buongiorno.*" She begins talking in Italian, her arm gesturing toward the window. I nod, even though I don't know what she's saying. She crosses the room and pulls open the curtains, letting in bright sunshine. I glance at the clock and realize I've slept until nearly ten in the morning. No wonder Luca's not here.

I'm naked again as Roberta holds up a robe, and I get out of bed to slip it on. "Where is Luca?"

Roberta says something in Italian, but I don't understand her. I'm really going to have to learn this language. As Roberta fusses around the room, I go into the restroom where I shower and get ready for the day. Going to the closet, I find a pretty pale green dress and slip it on.

When I consider all the effort Luca has gone through to ensure I have a full closet of clothes, my concerns about his intentions slip away. I don't know what he sees for the future between us, but this isn't just some casual little affair.

Roberta says something to me, and I'm able to understand the word *breakfast*. I follow her out of the room and back down to the dining room where a breakfast buffet is set up. In broken Italian, I ask her if Luca will be joining me for breakfast. She shakes her head and tells me, "No."

I pick up a plate and look at my choices for breakfast. I'm reminded that Italian breakfast is much different from at home in the United States. Italians don't generally eat savory foods like eggs and bacon. With a morning coffee, they have sweet items like cookies or pastries. I see an assortment of different options along with fruit, and a variety of spreads such as hazelnut chocolate and jams.

I select a brioche-looking pastry and some fruit. I'm taking it over to the table where a cup of cappuccino is already awaiting me when the doors to the dining room burst open and a woman strides in looking like she stepped out of a Vogue magazine. She's tall and lean with blonde hair that I'm sure isn't natural but doesn't look harsh. She's wearing cream-colored slacks and a silk shirt. She pushes large sunglasses up on her head as she approaches me. She's speaking Italian a mile a minute as she embraces me, giving me a kiss on each cheek. I stare at her in confusion. Who is she? God! Luca isn't married, is he?

Roberta says something to the woman who stops mid-statement. She turns her attention to me and asks, "You don't speak Italian?"

I shrug, feeling like it's an insult to them that I can't speak their language. "Only a little. "*Un pocco*," I say to show I know a few words.

The woman arches a brow. "Well, we'll need to work on that, won't we?" She gives me a large smile. "I'm Bianca Fontana. I'm married to Gino, one of Don Conte's caporegimes."

"I'm Aria Leone." I think I should shake her hand but remember we've already greeted each other with cheek kisses.

The woman lets out a laugh. "Oh, I know who you are, and you and I are going to be good friends." She moves over toward the buffet, picking up a plate and selecting something for breakfast. Clearly, she feels at home in Luca's home.

"I've been eager to meet you for some time."

Has Luca told others about me? That knowledge works to alleviate my doubt that he sees me only as a temporary plaything.

Bianca moves to the table and sits down, asking Roberta for something in Italian. When she looks at me, she says, "Sit. We have so much to talk about."

I sit to eat breakfast and listen as Bianca prattles on about her and the other wives.

"We all know you are a Mafia princess from the United States, but I've decided that I'm going to help you understand being a Mafia wife in Italy."

"Oh, but Luca and I aren't married." The rest of my doubt vanishes because if she knows about me from Luca and is talking marriage, surely, that means he sees me as his future wife. That knowledge fills me with happiness.

Bianca looks up at me from her espresso and blinks. "Oh, I see." She waves her hand. "I guess I just assumed. I mean, Don Conte went to so much trouble to bring you here." She leans forward conspiratorially. "Your brother is known, even here. For Don Conte to risk so much..." She lets her thought hang.

I realize I hadn't completely thought through this situation. Yes, I knew that Nico didn't approve of my being with Luca. I did run away, after all. But I hadn't considered the full ramifications of what that would mean between Luca and Nico. Had my actions started a potential war?

"But we won't think about that. You and I are going to have a full day of it." She raises her hand and snaps her fingers. Roberta is immediately at her side. Bianca starts talking to her in rapid Italian, and I have no clue what she's saying.

I eat my breakfast and drink my coffee as I watch the exchange. I study Bianca and how so well put together she is. I like to think that I dress well and look presentable, but I don't think I reach the level of Bianca's style and sophistication. She's immaculate in every way, from her clothes, her nails and her hair, her jewelry... all of her. I wonder if she has a stylist.

When breakfast is over, Bianca ushers me out the door toward a little red sports car. "First we will go to a spa. Nails and hair. And then we'll go shopping."

Roberta follows us out, speaking in Italian. Bianca ignores her. "Did Don Conte give you a credit card?"

I shake my head. "But I have my own money—"

Bianca shakes her head. "That won't do." She turns to Roberta, saying something to her in Italian. Roberta finally throws up her arms and retreats into the house.

"It'll be just a minute." Bianca waits by the car. Roberta reappears and hands me a wad of cash. I stare down at it and then at Bianca.

"You're Don Conte's woman now. Plus, I'm pretty sure he wouldn't want you using your own credit cards." She leans toward me again. "People can trace you that way."

"Who's tracing me?"

Her face contorts in confusion. "You ran away from your brother, didn't you?"

That unsettling feeling fills me again. I know my brother well enough to know that he will trace me. He'll likely come looking for me.

Had I just created a situation in which my brother and Luca are pitted against each other?

Two lethal men who are willing to kill to protect their own?

9

LUCA

Exiting the bed once Aria is asleep is no easy feat. I'd much rather hold her in my arms, maybe even make love to her in the middle of the night when she is soft and sleepy. But there's too much going on to indulge my urges.

After a night at the port with Bruno reviewing everything that happened yesterday and getting updates on Sabini and his men's whereabouts and activities, I'm walking back into my villa with Bruno close at hand. I want to immediately find Aria, partly to make sure she's still here, but mostly to take her back to bed. My body is still burning with the memory of being inside her, her lips around my cock. But my work isn't done.

The minute I walk into the door, Roberta comes flying toward me, her words firing off and her arms flailing. Immediately, I tense, wondering what is wrong.

"Ms. Leone isn't here," she says in Italian. "I had to go to the safe and get her some money."

"Why?" I can't imagine Roberta helping Aria escape or helping Niko help Aria escape.

Roberta takes a step back, an indication that I'm scaring her. "Mrs. Fontana arrived this morning. She whisked her off, demanding that I give Ms. Leone your credit card. I gave her money instead."

The tension in my chest releases. "Thank you for letting me know." I dismiss her, and she scurries off. I'm not worried about Bianca Fontana doing anything against me. I trust her more than I trust her husband, one of my capos. She's the epitome of a good Mafia wife, and it will be good for Aria to have a female friend while she's here in Italy. I am grateful, though, that Roberta didn't give Bianca my credit card. Who the hell knows what sort of thing she would've had Aria buy with it.

I head straight to my office with Bruno behind me.

"What is your plan with Don Leone's sister?" he asks as he closes the door behind him.

Deep down, I'd hoped that Niko would come around and approve of my marrying his sister. But after the call yesterday, I'm doubtful that it will happen. So, there's no reason to wait to claim her legally. "I'm going to marry her. Just a small, private ceremony. In a church."

Bruno arches a brow. He knows I'm not particularly religious, even though I was raised Catholic. My mother had been devout, not that it saved her from a terminal illness when I was just a boy. My father took his faith seriously as well. The irony of the life we lead contrasted with the teachings of the church doesn't escape me. But I've already considered how important tradition was to my father. That included the church. But it's not just my parents I'm thinking of honoring by having a church wedding. I think a woman who saved herself for one man is likely to want an official wedding ceremony.

"You have a problem with that?" I ask Bruno.

He shakes his head with a smirk on his face. "Not at all. Will we be inviting Don Leone and his family?"

"No. This marriage needs to be legitimate and official, but it also needs to be done in the next few days. I need you to go talk to Father Pagano and set it up. Make a big donation to the church, and I'm sure it won't be a problem." I sit behind my desk.

"Father Pagano is always happy to be of service to you."

"Make the donation, anyway." If there is a God, perhaps this will be a mark in my favor to offset all the negative marks against me.

Bruno gives a single nod. "What about the other thing?"

"I want eyes and ears on Sabini and all his men for the time being. I have a feeling with his man gone missing, he'll play it safe—"

"I don't know. He's gotten pretty brazen."

I nod, acknowledging that Enzo Sabini is dumb enough not to take the hint. But he's got a few smart men around him who'll likely advise holding back or playing it safe. It's time for me to start playing offense. "Sabini thinks he can fuck with my business, so let's go ahead and fuck with his." Although my Family and the Sabini Family have a long history of rivalry, my father and Enzo's father had a truce of sorts. In the political arena, it would have been called a treaty. But Enzo broke that, which means I can now take what I want from him.

"Let's start infiltrating his territories. Be discreet. I don't want him to see us coming or know that we're there until his ass is against the wall and I can finally end him and take what's his."

Bruno nods.

Sabini is something I need to deal with, but he's not my only concern at the moment. I also need to consider what Niko's next steps might be.

"I also need eyes and ears for any ways that Niko Leone might retaliate."

"He's a bit limited on what he can do from New York."

"We're talking about his sister here. I can't rule out that he'll come to Italy. And of course, mine isn't the only business he's connected to here. I don't want to take any chances. Not until Aria and I are married and this is settled."

Bruno is quiet, but his stare speaks volumes.

"What?" I ask, sitting back in my chair.

"It's possible that all this is going to cause war."

I arch a brow. "Are you afraid of Niko Leone?"

Bruno's eyes narrow. "I'd be a fool not to be. His power doesn't stretch over here, but he's powerful in the United States."

He's right. I'm not afraid of Niko, but I'm not so arrogant to think that he can't find a way to hurt me. "At this point, I have the advantage. Aria is with me. What is that they say in the United States? Possession is nine-tenths of the law?"

Bruno gives a half-shrug. "What if he goes to Sabini for help?"

I let out a laugh. "Niko is not dumb enough to do that. He'll see Sabini as being as ineffective and stupid as I do. He's not going to put his sister's life in his hands."

"And what about his sister? I get the feeling that she's not aware of the world we live in. Do you think she's going to choose you over her brother?"

"I guess we'll find out." A good man would give Aria a choice. I'm not a good man. But I also know that if I'm going to have the sort of wife my father spoke about, I need Aria on my side.

She won't do me any good if I keep her against her will, even as I know that I could absolutely do that. I need to tread carefully and give her the fairytale she wants if I'm going to keep her on my side.

Remembering that she's with Bianca Fontana, I ask Bruno about Gino, her husband. Bruno rolls his eyes because he feels about Gino the way I do. Gino is about thirty years older than Bianca. The marriage is all about sex for him and money for her. Admittedly, Bianca is a good trophy wife. She understands what being a Mafia wife means, something I hope she can help Aria navigate.

But Gino is one of the old guards of my father's and I don't completely trust him. Not that he'd betray me because I don't believe he would. While he might not respect me like he did my father, he was devoted to my father and my father put his trust in me. So, Gino goes along in honor of my father. Still, I'm not convinced that Gino doesn't take a little on the side, or that his affinity for women and substances hasn't made him a liability.

"He's in Rome," Bruno informs me. "He and his men are keeping an eye on Sabini's men there as well. At least when he's not off fucking that mistress of his."

"It's probably time we make a trip to Rome." It's not something that I want to do right now, but Gino tends to respond better when I deal with him in person than over the phone.

"Anyone else you want to be there?" Bruno asks.

"Bring in all the capos in the region."

Bruno nods. "When do you want to meet?"

I want to put it off. I finally have Aria here, and I want to bury myself in that sweet body of hers again. But this business needs attending to.

"The first thing tomorrow. "

"And what about this wedding? How soon do we need to set that up?"

"I want it done by the end of the week."

Bruno nods and exits my office.

I settle in at my desk to do what I do best, run a lucrative, albeit illegal, business. But Aria isn't far from my mind. I check my watch and have half a mind to send somebody out to find her and bring her back home.

But I'm a man who tries hard not to give in to urges and impulses.

A lack of control is a sign of weakness, and there's one thing no one will ever say about me and that is that Luca Conte is weak. I suppose that's another lesson my father taught me. Patience.

In patience and self-control is where power lies. It's a power that I wield effectively. Enzo won't see it coming when I finally take him down. And if Niko is smart, he won't test me. He'll see what I can offer Aria and him and give his blessing.

But if not, I'm prepared to defend what's mine. To keep what's mine. To keep Aria.

10

ARIA

Spending the day with Bianca is a bit like being on a roller coaster ride. Especially the way she drives her little sports car. Fast and thrilling, but a little scary as well.

The first part of the day is all about pampering. Nails, hair, and a massage. Next, we shop at the boutique couture stores where Bianca purchases something from each and every one we enter. Since I already have a closet full of new clothes, I only splurge on a handbag.

Now we're sitting at a café having coffee and more pastries.

"I want to hear all about your great escape to come to Luca," she says, her dark eyes attentive on me like she really is interested in my story.

"Luca and I were exchanging secret notes through a bookstore."

Bianca's eyes light with delight as she leans forward, resting her chin on her palm, listening intently.

"Then one day, I got a note asking me to run away. He made all the flight arrangements, but it was up to me to get to the airport. My brother is very protective, so it wasn't easy."

Bianca nods. "I have slipped my bodyguards a time or two." She glances over to the corner of the room where two dark suited men sit. They make me think of Italian FBI men, but I know they are in fact made men.

"I was able to sneak out of the house and order a car that got me to the airport. Luca's man, Bruno, was there, and he escorted me over."

Bianca let out a long sigh. "That's so romantic."

"How did you and your husband meet?"

She straightens and waves a hand. "It is not so romantic. What Gino and I have doesn't involve love. Not that we're not happy. We both get what we want."

I frown. "You didn't want to marry for love?"

Her eyes narrow, making her look shrewd. "I can get love elsewhere. But the luxuries in life that I enjoy, for that I need Gino."

This is not a surprise to me. I'm well aware that many of the marriages in the Mafia have nothing to do with love. Often, they are business or political moves.

I've always known that I didn't want that. Especially after I saw how much Niko loved Elena, I was sure that he would support me in marrying for love. I wish I understood why he is so against Luca.

"You knew about me before I arrived," I say, wondering how good of friends she is with Luca.

Her eyes sparkle. "As wives, we learn a great deal from pillow talk. Gino spent a lot of time talking about the American woman Luca was pining over."

Pining? My smile at hearing this is probably a little goofy, but I don't care. Thinking of Luca pining over me fills me with joy.

"So, of course, all were curious about you. And then I heard you arrived, and so I came over first thing. And now here we are, becoming fast friends."

Bianca is a woman who clearly enjoys the finer things in life and has a few shallow traits, but she is friendly and right now, my only friend in Italy.

She checks her watch and then quickly grabs her purse. "We must get going." She pays the bill, and her stiletto heels click on the tiles as we walk out of the café. As we walk to her car, a group of young men starts whistling and talking to us. I suppose it's the Italian equivalent of catcalls.

Bianca smiles coyly. "It is nice when men appreciate a beautiful woman, don't you think?"

I have to admit, it doesn't feel quite as creepy from these men as it does from the men I experience in New York. As we reach her car, I open the door to get in, noticing a man across the street whose phone appears to be pointed in our direction. I turn to look behind me to see what he might be trying to take a picture of, but it's just a building.

As I get in the car, I ask, "Is it normal for them to take pictures?"

"Once they know who you are, no one would dare to do it. Luca is one of the most feared men in the country."

I have a flash of memory of the man on his knees begging Luca for his life.

She puts the car in gear, and we zoom off like we're on the interstate, not a narrow, crowded city road. My fingers clutch my seat, and I send a silent prayer up that we don't end up crumpled in a heap.

The guards allow us to enter Luca's property, and Bianca parks at the front door. She leans over, giving me a kiss on each cheek. "We'll see each other soon."

"Thank you, Bianca. I had a lot of fun today."

She beams at me, and I suspect she wants me to tell Luca about her good deeds.

I exit the car and enter the house, stopping short when I see Luca standing at the base of the stairs as if he's waiting for me. I study him, trying to decipher what he might be thinking. Is he upset that I went out?

His body looks relaxed, but his brows narrow as he stares at me. "Did you have a good time with Bianca?"

I nod, moving toward him, but not in any hurry as I'm still trying to figure out his feelings. "She's very nice."

He gives a single nod. "I'm glad you think so. She will be a good friend to you. She will help you fit into our world here."

His gaze is still intense, which unsettles me. His head tilts to the side. "Did you have your hair done?"

Nervously, I run my fingers through the ends of my hair. "Not really. Just a little styling."

He steps in front of me, and his fingers run up the back of my neck, threading through my hair. Then he tugs me in, and his lips cover mine in a fierce, bruising kiss that heats my blood to infernal levels.

When he pulls away, I say, "Well, hello to you too."

His lips twitch up slightly. "You should see Bianca again tomorrow and tell her to take you out to buy a suitable wedding dress."

It takes a moment for my brain to register his words. When it does, my jaw drops. "What?"

"A wedding dress. I have already disrespected Niko by stealing you away and taking you to my bed. I would much prefer not to have him as an enemy, if I can help it. So, we must marry. I'm making arrangements for us to have a wedding at the church that my parents married in."

I'm in shock. I'm elated, wondering why I was so worried about his intentions toward me earlier in the day. At the same time, something feels off. I realize that he is not asking me. He is telling me.

His knuckles brush along my cheek, and the sizzle it sends through my skin distracts me. "Unless you changed your mind about me, *Mio Angelo.*"

My head moves from side to side indicating that no, I haven't changed my mind.

His expression is soft, even caring. "Are you still sore from yesterday?"

I give a half shrug. "It's not bad."

"I have thought about nothing except having you in my bed again." He sweeps me up to his arms and starts walking upstairs. That niggle of uncertainty remains, but it's competing with the feelings of love and how romantic this all is. What woman doesn't want to be swept off her feet by a man who knows what he wants and wants to claim it?

In his room, he sets me by the bed and kisses me as his hands roam my body, removing my clothes as he goes. There's something about his kiss, his touch, that empties my mind of everything but him and how he makes me feel. Cherished. Desired. Sexy.

When I'm naked, he steps back, his gaze raking over my body. His eyes fill with a wild fire as he tugs at his tie. "Get on the bed."

I sit and scoot back until I can fully lie down. I watch him, admiring his strong body as his clothes fall away. He pushes his pants down, and his dick springs free, already thick and hard.

"You like what you see?" His voice is low, husky.

"Yes."

He climbs over me. Straddling my body, he guides his dick to my mouth. "And what do you taste?"

I'm self-conscious because I'm not well-versed in the acts of sex, but I go with instinct and snake my tongue out. It's not like I haven't used my mouth on him before. It's just that this position is different, a little scary as I feel caged in.

"Don't worry, *Mio Angelo*. I won't hurt you." He presses himself inside my mouth. Instinctively, my hands go to his thighs, needing to make sure he doesn't choke me. Beyond that, I try to make him happy as he slowly moves in and out of my mouth.

A moment later, he slips out and moves down my body enough to rub his dick over my breasts. "I have much to teach you about the pleasures of the flesh." His tip flicks over my nipple, sending an electric shock to my pussy. "Do you want to learn?"

I nod.

"Good." He moves off me. "Get on your knees. Put your hands on the headboard."

I do as he asks, still feeling uncertain and at the same time, wanting to make him happy. I look over my shoulder, wondering what he's going to do.

He moves in behind me, his hands on my hips as he strings kisses along my shoulder. "Relax." His hands move around me, cupping my breasts, pinching my nipples as he continues to suck and kiss my neck.

I let out a breath, and with it, the tension from uncertainty. It's replaced by a new tension growing in my center. I let out a moan as he kneads my nipples.

"That's right," he whispers. One hand slides down my belly and to my folds. "So wet for me."

His finger rubs my clit, and my hips rock.

"I'm going to fuck you this way, Aria. From behind."

"Okay." I grip the headboard, not sure what to expect, and yet, I am burning up. I need him inside me.

He rubs his dick through my folds. The soft, velvety feel of him sends more sparks through me. Instinctively, I arch back, wanting him to stop teasing me.

"Luca." His name escapes on a gasp.

"Yes? What do you need?" He does it again, and the frustration is unbearable.

"You..."

"Me what?"

"Inside me. Please." My hips are shaking. It's shocking how quickly my need has built.

"Tell me to fuck you."

I imagine if I wasn't in a state of utterly aroused desperation, I'd roll my eyes at this request. Men can be so weird when it comes to needing to feel macho. But at this point, I'll do anything.

"Fuck me." I barely have the word out when he drives in so hard it pushes me forward.

"Say it again." His voice is demanding.

"Fuck me."

He growls as he withdraws and plunges in again. The friction of him inside me is maddeningly spectacular.

"Say my name." He withdraws and stills.

My pussy is pulsing with need. I whimper as it's nearly painful. "Fuck me, Luca."

"Yes!" He drives in again, and this time, he rocks in and out of me, fast, faster until I'm gasping and my pussy is on fire.

"Oh, my God..." I grip the headboard, worried that I'm about to shatter.

"Do you feel me fucking you, Aria?" His breath is harsh on my neck.

I try to say yes, but a moan escapes instead.

"You gave this to me, did you not? I'm the only man who's been in your sweet pussy."

"Yes... oh, God, Luca."

"Fuck... I'm so fucking close. Come, Aria. Come on my cock."

His words take me the rest of the way. My orgasm slams into me, crashing through like a tsunami. My entire body shakes, shudders.

"Yes... fuck, yes..." He chants the words as he thrusts in, grinds against me, and warmth fills me. By the time he finishes, I'm not sure how I'm still able to be on my knees gripping the headboard. My body feels completely boneless.

He pulls away, collapsing on the bed beside me. I'm wobbly as I maneuver myself to lie down next to him. I snuggle up to him, letting myself completely relax. As I rest with my head on his shoulder, the doubts I had about his feelings for me are nearly nonexistent. After all, he wants to marry me.

Marriage. God. The idea of it is crazy, right? It's too soon, too fast. I feel like I'm on a freight train, barreling down the tracks, nearly out of control. It's terrifying, and at the same time, exciting. I feel so alive. So in control of my own life. Oh, sure, I'll be bound by the rules of Mafia life, but I made this choice. I feel freer than I have in a long time. Free and blissfully happy.

"When we started exchanging those notes, I had no idea that I'd end up here," I say as I rest my hand over his chest, feeling his heartbeat.

He puts one arm behind his head, looking like he doesn't have a care in the world. "You doubted me?"

"Not at all." I nestle up closer to him, inhaling his scent. "It's turned out perfect. How did you manage the notes from Italy?"

"You do what you have to do to get what you want." His tone is dismissive as if he doesn't want to talk about it.

I tilt my head up to look at him, to see what the expression on his face might tell me. "It was very romantic."

His eyes cast down toward me. "Like I said, you do what you have to do."

I frown, laying my head back down on his shoulder. "Well, I suppose it's up in the air whether Niko will come to the wedding, but Lucy, and Elena, and maybe even Kate will come for sure." Well, maybe not Elena if Niko doesn't allow her. But I know they're happy for me.

He pulls away from me abruptly, and I thump down on the bed as he stands and goes to put on his clothes. "They won't be coming."

I sit up, pulling the sheet up to cover myself. "Why not?"

"For one, there won't be enough time."

"Maybe we could push it back. What's the hurry?"

He steps into his slacks. "Niko is the hurry."

"I'll talk to him. Since we're getting married, he'll see that what we have is real."

He slips his shirt on, buttoning just the bottom buttons before tucking it into his waistband. "I doubt it."

"He's stubborn, but—"

"Are you that naïve?" He stands at the end of the bed with his hands on his hips, staring at me with an expression that suggests he thinks I'm stupid. It's not a nice feeling.

"Is it possible that you really do not understand what's going on here? I asked for Niko's permission, and he outright refused. My notes luring you here, your being here, that's an act of war. We are not living inside some sort of fairytale, Aria. Your brother and I are two very powerful men who don't take kindly to someone else infringing on what's theirs. As far as your brother is concerned, I'm a dead man. And if he sets foot anywhere near me or you, he's a dead man. You do understand this, don't you?"

My body trembles as fear—no, terror—fills me. For a moment, I can't breathe. It's not that I don't understand the Mafia world, because I do. Mostly.

It's just that I think the rules are different for families. That Niko cared about me enough to want my happiness. That Luca would feel the same.

I begin to believe that Luca is right to think I'm naïve or stupid because I'm realizing that Luca's attention, his desire to marry me, has nothing to do with love and everything to do with power.

I can't do much to help him here in Italy, where he is already the most powerful Don in the country. But I can help him gain a foothold in New York.

My heart cracks, and I feel like the biggest idiot in the world. I'm a pawn for Luca's ambition.

My voice quavers as I ask, "Do you even care about me?"

He lets out what sounds like an explicative, but it's in Italian so I'm not sure. "I wouldn't have gone through all the trouble to get you here if I didn't care about you. Now that you are here, you've made your choice, and I've staked my claim." He tilts his head to the side and looks as if he's thinking for a moment. Then he moves toward me, crawling on the bed like a prowling cat until I fall back and he's over me, caging me in. He tugs the sheet down, his hand blatantly running down my body, cupping my breast and squeezing it. I gasp, responding even though I don't want to.

"Have I not treated you well, *Mio Angelo*?"

I give a small nod because it's true.

"I'm prepared to give you the world. To have you by my side and grant your every wish." He's saying the words every woman wants to hear, but I can tell by the tone of his voice that there are conditions.

"I'm well within my right to make you stay, but just this once, and only this once, I'm going to give you the choice again. It's either me or Niko." His fingers pinch my nipple, making it hard for me to think. It's probably what he wants.

"Why do I have to choose?"

"You know why." He dips his head, his lips wrapping around my nipple, sucking gently, coaxing me into submission. I should fight it, but it feels so good. My hand automatically threads into his hair and pulls him to me, keeping him on my breast.

"You can have a future as the younger sister of a powerful Mafia Don who will hide you away in a gilded cage. Or you can be with me, reign as the queen you are by my side." His lips trail down my body, pushing the sheet further away as he insinuates himself between my thighs.

I know this is wrong. I should stop this, but I arch, offering myself to him. His mouth covers my pussy, and everything but the most delicious sensations he sends through me evaporates. Despite having a mind-blowing orgasm already, within minutes, another one hits me, sending me scattering to the wind.

My breath hasn't yet returned to normal as he backs off the bed and stands, grabbing his tie and wrapping it around his neck. "Think about your choice carefully, *Mio Angelo*. Should you choose your brother, I will have you on a plane home and you will never see me again. And if you choose me, as I hope you will because I do care about you, it's possible you'll never set foot in New York again."

His piercing, dark eyes watch me for a moment. "I have to go to Rome for a day or two. You have until then to decide." He grabs his coat and exits the room.

I lie in bed stunned at the turn of events. If he cared for me, wouldn't he want me to be happy and to be able to see my family?

Then again, he's probably right and Niko will be out for Luca's life. Or Niko will declare me dead to him for running away. That's how stupid this Mafia world can sometimes be.

I let out a frustrated growl and punch the bed. Luca's seduction manipulated me, and I'd allowed it. But that is only because I love him. Despite everything, including my better judgment, by his side is where I want to be.

He's right that by returning to Niko, I will continue to be sheltered, not allowed to live a full life. No doubt, there will be limitations on me with Luca, as well, but he doesn't see me as something to hide away. He wants to elevate me, make me a part of his life. As much as I love Niko, for my life to move forward, the choice is clear. The choice is Luca.

11

LUCA

I'm a decisive man. To get what I want, I can manipulate seductively or coerce forcefully. I chose the former on Aria, and as I leave her, I feel certain that she'll choose me as her future.

But there's an unsettling feeling in the pit of my stomach. It almost feels like my conscience is chastising me for manipulating her. I push it away as I head downstairs, situating my tie in place and going on the hunt for Roberta.

I find her in the kitchen, conferring with a book. "I'm going to Rome. I hope it will only be for tonight, but it may be more than that. It's your job to keep an eye on Aria. Keep her comfortable and happy, but she's only to leave with Bianca, understood? Have Bianca take her shopping for a wedding dress."

Roberta nods. "*Si, Don Conte.*"

When I return to the foyer, Bruno is waiting. "The car is ready to go to Rome."

I make a beeline for the front door, which Bruno opens, and I stride out ready to conquer the world, or at the very least, Sabini.

When we arrive in Rome, I have my driver take Bruno and me to the butcher shop that my family has owned for over a century, long before my great-grandfather became a Mafia Don. I promised my father I'd keep it, as it was one of those things that represented tradition. It's a legitimately run business, except for the secret room in the basement where I often meet with my men. That's where I head to now.

When I get there, all the capos from the area are already waiting. As I enter the room, Gino Fontana gives me a knowing smirk like a fourteen-year-old boy with a hard on, which, his being a sixty-something-year-old man, makes him look like a pervert. "Bianca likes your new pet better than the other one."

My fingers itch to grab my gun and put a bullet in his forehead.

Leonardo, a contemporary of Gino's, has the same disgusting smirk on his face as he grabs his crotch. "Maybe now the boss will share Electra with us. I wouldn't mind her mouth around —"

This time, I do pull out my gun and hold it toward them both. "Is this the type of thing you do while on the job for me? Jerk off?"

Leonardo has enough smarts to bow his head. "*Mi dispiace, Don Conte.*"

Gino crosses his arms over his chest but keeps his mouth shut.

I set my gun on the desk as a reminder that I'm not the sort of man who puts up with a bunch of bullshit.

Bruno goes to stand behind the two men, at which point Gino drops his arms.

I stand behind my desk, inventorying each of my men one by one. "I'm getting married this weekend. You are invited, and you can bring your wives. And I mean wives. None of your mistresses or playthings. For those of you who aren't married, you are to bring a respectable woman. We're marrying in a church. *Avete capito?*"

My men nod.

"Congratulations, Don Conte," Leonardo says. "May your marriage be happy and filled with healthy, beautiful children."

Inwardly, I roll my eyes at his suck up, but I nod and then sit down. "Sabini's looking to make some moves. I want to find out what, if anything, you've seen since he sent that dead motherfucker to my dock."

"They're trying to be subtle, but they stand out as obvious as my dick—" Gino stops himself as if he realizes being crass probably isn't the right way to move forward. "Let's just say they're easy to spot. Mostly, they seem to be casing. Me and Leonardo followed a couple, and we think we found where some of them might be hiding."

"Sabini thinks Rome is his, so his center base is likely here. But like a spiderweb, he's trying to move throughout Rome and beyond into my space. That's going to stop. You keep your eyes and ears open, and don't do anything unless there's an act against me. You understand?"

My men nod. "Bruno, Carlo, and Paolo, I want you to return the favor. I want you to see where Sabini's weak and we can walk in and take it." They nod their heads as well.

I have each of my capos check in, reporting about their duties and the men who operate underneath them. By the time I finish, it's nearly eleven, but my night is unfinished.

I get into my waiting car, and Bruno slides in with me. "When are you finally going to take out that motherfucker Gino?" he asks.

My lips twitch upward knowing my second-in-command would happily take care of it for me if I wanted. "It won't be long before he either strokes out while one of his mistresses sucks his dick or someone else will take him out for us."

Bruno shakes his head. "Your father's gone."

"But he trusted Gino. I can't go against my father, dead or not. But I won't cry any tears when Gino is gone."

Several moments later, my driver pulls up in front of one of my clubs. I'm happy to see that it's busy even on a weeknight. Being in Rome, it's a hotspot not just for Italians, but anyone of any nationality visiting the city.

Enough people know me and of my reputation, even though no law enforcement has ever been able to catch me. As a result, the crowd parts like the Red Sea for me. That is, except for a few tourists, but I don't mind. My men easily maneuver them aside as I make my way to my usual table.

Just before I get to it, Electra appears before me. She's not a dancer anymore now that I made her the dancer supervisor. So, she's not dressed quite as provocatively as she used to be. Instead of a skintight dress, she's wearing one that fits looser in a dark color. That isn't to say that her tits aren't nearly falling out of the bodice. They seem larger, which is saying something. Even so, I'm not tempted.

Electra makes her way to me, her eyes filled with the promise of a great blow job, and there was a time when I would have dropped my pants willingly. But since meeting Aria, I've lost all interest in Electra, or any women, actually.

I suppose it's my fault that she continues to think she can become my wife, or at the very least, my mistress. I never outright told her that we were done. I guess I was keeping my options open in case Aria didn't come to me.

Electra's finger draws down my tie and then wraps around it. "I thought maybe you forgot about me, Don Conte." She licks her lips. "I've been so thirsty for you."

My dick stays still in my pants, not tempted even a little. I wrap my hand over hers. "You're welcome to find someone else to sate your thirst." I tug her hand away. "Find Carmine and send him to my table."

I sit, and my drink appears, scotch on the rocks.

Carmine, the club's manager, arrives and sits at the table. "*Buonasera, Don Conte.*"

"I need you to be extra alert. At least from now until the weekend. My bride-to-be's brother may come or send some of his men to try and take what's now mine. Bruno here will give you photos."

Carmen bows his head. "Of course." Behind him, Electra's brows furrow, a mixture of shock and anger, but I ignore it.

"I'm asking all the clubs to be extra vigilant, but I also want you all to talk together. It's possible they'll take a divide and conquer approach."

"We'll keep an eye out." Carmine takes the photos I have of Niko, Donovan, Lucy, and Liam, along with a few other of his men.

"*Grazie*, Carmine."

Recognizing I've dismissed him, he stands, ready to return to work.

"Take Electra with you," I order.

He grips her upper arm and tugs her away. She's smart enough not to argue.

"Speak of the fucking devil," Bruno says, nodding toward the bar.

I turn to see Gino, his eyes on Electra and his hand snaking down to his groin.

I down my drink. "If there's anybody that can give Gino a deadly stroke, it will be Electra sucking his cock." She really is good at it, but Aria... God, when her lips wrapped around my dick, I was the one nearly stroking out.

I rise and make my way to the door to call it a night. I ask my driver to take me to my apartment in town, leaving Bruno to go to his place.

Once home, I take my clothes off and lie in bed, doing my damnedest to resist the urge to call Aria. For one, it's late, and she's probably still adjusting to the time change. But two, I can't give in to these urges to want to hear her voice.

But the image of her sucking me off. Of how her ass looked as I fucked her today... that urge can't be brushed off. I really thought that once she arrived, I wouldn't need to deal with such things. But my dick has other ideas.

I push the sheets down, exposing my naked body. I wrap my hand around my dick, stroking fast and then slow. I think about her, not just sexually, but how she's going to be mine. I have no doubt she'll choose me.

Thinking of the power that she and I are going to wield together excites me until my cum shoots like a fountain onto my chest.

After a quick shower, I climb back into bed, placing my hands behind my head and smiling. Is it an American saying about the world being my oyster? It's definitely mine, and Aria is my pearl.

12

ARIA

I don't sleep well. The conversation I had with Luca before he left and my current situation play over and over again in my mind. My decision to stay has been made, but it isn't like I have good choices to choose from. When I wake up this morning, I wonder if there is a third option.

As Roberta opens my curtains to greet the day, a part of me wants to stay in bed because what is there for me to do? I'm supposed to be getting a wedding dress, but to be honest, I'm not excited about the life it appears I'll have here.

I suppose I've set myself up for this disappointment, carrying on with fantasies of true love. Luca went to all this work to get me here. He even moved me into his bedroom. But he's been gone more than he's been here. The only time he spends with me is to have sex. Is that all he wants from me?

I'm really confused. On the one hand, he says he cares for me and wants to marry me, albeit only to appease Niko, but then he seems disinterested in me except for sex.

I drag myself from bed, showering and getting dressed. I make my way downstairs to the dining room, where cappuccino waits along with a buffet of breakfast pastries.

I've just sat down to eat when Bianca sweeps into the room. "*Ciao, Amica*. We're going shopping today for a wedding dress. You have to show me your ring." She sits down next to me and takes my hand. She frowns when she sees the unadorned ring finger and looks up into my face.

I shrug. "No ring."

She sits back, her eyes narrowing. "Is there a baby?"

I shake my head. Granted, Luca hasn't used any protection, but I've been on the pill for many years simply because I like the convenience of knowing when my period is coming every month.

She studies me for a moment. "He must've asked you in the spur of the moment, in the heat of passion, right?"

I nod because I don't want her pity at learning Luca didn't ask me to marry him out of love but commanded it to keep my brother at bay.

"You are the envy of women all throughout Italy. You won the heart of Luca Conte." She stands and goes to make herself a plate.

I remember Luca telling me to call Bianca about shopping. I didn't call her, so I wonder if he did. Or maybe he had Roberta call her.

Bianca returns to the table with her food. "We will go buy a dress, and then you will come out to my place. I'm having a little afternoon party. You'll be able to meet the other wives."

Reality descends on me. I'm about to be a Mafia wife. And not just any Mafia wife but the wife of the most powerful Don in the country. Not long ago, the idea of that felt like a fairy tale, marrying into royalty, but today, the weight of it unsettles me. If only I could know for sure that Luca loves me. That he is marrying me for me, and not simply as a defensive move against my brother.

After breakfast, Bianca leads me out to a waiting sedan. "Today, Ernesto drives. We have many shops to go to."

We sit in the back of the car as her driver, Ernesto, takes us into town. The first stop is a bridal boutique.

"You're marrying in the church where Luca's parents married. Luca's father very much liked tradition. It's nice that Luca is honoring him in this way."

It's information like this that reminds me of the deeper, more feeling person that Luca can be. What I don't know is whether it's authentic or just the politics of Mafia life.

I try on the first dress, a white, lacy, fitted dress that is traditional but pretty. I study myself in the mirror, trying not to show how unhappy I am that this isn't an exciting moment that I'd dreamed of. Elena, Lucy, and Kate should be here, not Bianca.

Behind me, Bianca frowns. "You don't seem very happy for a bride-to-be."

I don't know Bianca well enough to share my inner turmoil. I give her a wan smile. "I guess I'm still jet lagged."

She nods. "When we finish shopping, I'll take you to my beach house. We'll have wine and be with the other wives. It will cheer you up."

I try on several dresses and finally pick one Bianca liked the most. After that, we go to a shop to buy lingerie. She tries to take me to buy a trousseau, but I tell her that Luca has already bought me a whole closet of clothes.

It's nearly noon when Ernesto drives us out to Bianca's house along the shore. I'm a little surprised as I walk in because it doesn't look like a place where a Mafia capo would live. It has Bianca written all over it with pink and white décor and two little dogs dressed in pink greeting her at the door.

She calls out to someone in Italian. The only word I recognize is vino. I could definitely use some wine.

She leads me out onto a terrace that has a lovely view of the ocean. I'm served a glass of wine as other guests arrive. Bianca introduces me to the wives of the men who work for the Conte family. They all scrutinize me but remain guarded and polite, probably because I'm about to marry the Don.

As the wine flows, the wives loosen up and I begin to learn a lot about their lives here in Italy. To be honest, it's not so different from the lives of Mafia wives back home. Mostly, they live to keep their husbands happy and on occasion get involved in business. It's a traditional life, but because they have money, they also are able to enjoy many of life's luxuries. It's not so different for Elena, although I know Niko works very hard to keep her happy, helping her indulge in her interests. Lucy is an entirely different kind of Mafia wife, one that I doubt would be allowed here in Italy where tradition is so important.

As I sit with these women, I see my future. It's not horrible, but I wonder if at some point it'll begin to feel tedious and small despite all the luxuries. Women here are still subservient to the whims of their powerful husbands. Because of the potential dangers in their world, they're not fully free and able to be spontaneous. This is how I grew up and how my life will be no matter whether I live here or in New York. But Luca has given me a choice of which gilded cage I prefer.

Bianca's housekeeper serves us a platter of antipasti, and wine keeps coming.

I don't miss the judgmental expressions of all the wives when they learn I can't converse in Italian, but they all agree to speak English.

"Alfredo is buying me a condo in Switzerland," Maria, a middle-aged, yet very chic, woman says in English.

"Out of love or guilt?" Allessa, a wife around Bianca's age, early thirties, asks.

Maria laughs. "I found out he bought one of his mistresses a diamond bracelet. So, of course, I used that. We should all plan a trip."

I stare at Maria, who doesn't seem at all concerned that her husband has a mistress. I expect the other women to console her or ask why she's still with him. Instead, they share all the gifts they've received from their husbands as a penance for infidelity.

I must be gaping because Bianca asks, "What is the matter, Aria?"

"I'm just so surprised to hear how you accept the fact that your husbands are unfaithful. Shouldn't you be angry and hurt?"

Bianca laughs. "How do you think I got this lovely villa that I have decorated in pink? Besides, I'm very happy that Gino has his girl-friends because he's old and fat and I don't like it when he touches me."

I'm in shock. "All of your husbands have a mistress?"

The ladies look at me like they wonder what the big deal is.

"You are young." Maria looks at me with a mixture of motherly wisdom and pity. "You still believe in fairy tales."

"It doesn't mean our husbands don't love us. But they have needs we can't always give, especially when they're doing business or travel-ing," Francesca, one of the other wives, states. Like Bianca, her tone suggests she isn't interested in having sex with her husband. Do they love these men?

"Of course, Don Conte might be different." Bianca's expression tells me she's just trying to be nice.

"His father was devoted to his wives," Maria adds.

Allessa laughs. "He couldn't perform for his last wife."

I perk up. "Lucy?"

They look at me, confused.

"Lucia?" I ask, remembering Lucy is the nickname we use. "My brother is married to her sister."

They exchange glances that I can't decipher. Did they not know Lucy returned to New York? That she was a co-boss with her husband, Donovan, in New Jersey?

"Yes, Lucia. She was good to Don Conte... Giuseppe." Bianca clarifies that she's referring to Luca's father. "I know Luca feels indebted to her for her kindness and friendship to his father."

"She's remarried, is she not?" Maria asks.

"I nod. Donovan. He's a good—"

"An Irishman?" Maria raises a brow.

"His last name is Ricci." I'm reminded that in Italy, they stick closer to the old ways, including only Italians in the Mafia. "They're expecting a baby." I'm not sure why I say that or even if it's wise. Does Lucy have enemies who would cross the ocean to try and hurt her or her baby?

"Do you have children?" I quickly ask to move the conversation along.

Maria and Alessa have two children. Francesca laments that she is likely expecting her fourth child. Perhaps that's why she seems to not like having sex with her husband.

The conversation continues about motherhood, but my mind reels about their acceptance of infidelity. Do all Mafia wives have to put up with this or just these ones? This, of course, leads me to wonder if Luca is faithful. Is he expecting me to accept that he'll have a woman on the side? God. Is he with another woman now? Is that why he stayed overnight in Rome?

I'm feeling sick. I rise from my chair to go get a glass of water.

"Is everything alright?" Bianca asks.

"I just want some water."

"I can have Rosa bring—"

"No, that's okay. I need to walk off this wine." I smile and hope they don't see how torn up I am.

I can't turn my mind off as I sip the water and contemplate my life. But I can't stand in the kitchen all day, so I make my way back to the terrace. When I return, the women are speaking Italian. I don't know what they're saying, but I recognize Luca's name. They stop talking abruptly, suggesting they were talking about me.

The women all look at Bianca expectantly.

"What?" I ask.

"They are concerned that your... expectations for marriage are naïve," Bianca says carefully.

Naïve? Isn't that what Luca called me?

"I told you what Luca went through to get me here, the risk he's taking by going against my brother. Why would he do that if he didn't love me? Only me." How odd that I'm defending him when my brain is filled with doubt.

Bianca nods. "Of course—"

"Show her, Bianca," Maria says.

"It doesn't prove anything. And I'm not about to upset Don Conte's betrothed. Are you?" Bianca's carefree façade cracks with nerves.

The women shirk back, which I take to be an expression of their fear of Luca. Would he hurt them? The image of the begging man returns. Just how brutal is Luca?

"Show me what?" I ask.

"It's nothing—"

"No. I want to know." My voice is bolder, demanding. I might be naïve, but I'm not a doormat.

Bianca purses her lips, but she pulls out her phone, poking at it. Then she hands it to me. The image on the screen shows Luca with a large-breasted woman who is pulling at his tie, and his hand is on hers. They appear to be in a club. My stomach sinks, but I suck in a breath to keep strong.

I look at the woman. "Luca is a powerful, handsome man. I'm sure women try to seduce him all the time."

All eyes are pitying me.

"That's Electra. She's been a plaything of Don Conte's for some time," Francesca says.

"It's well known that she wanted to be his wife," Maria adds.

Bianca makes a face. "She's trash. And you're right, Aria, it's possible she's just trying to get him back. She works at his club."

The women shake their heads, and I know Bianca is trying to make light of the situation. Inside, my heart is beating a million miles a minute. All my doubt is gone, replaced with surety that I made a mistake in coming here.

Bianca looks at the women knowingly.

"Bianca is right," Allesandra says. "Don Conte is a good man, like his father."

The rest of the women nod, but I know they're patronizing me. Probably because they worry what Luca will do if he finds out they told me about his mistress.

I try to brush it off because it's humiliating enough. "I'll make him forget her."

The ladies laugh. "That's the spirit."

I'm glad when I can leave without it looking like I'm running away. I wait until after a few other of the wives leave, then yawn and report that I'm still jet lagged.

Bianca asks Ernesto to take me home. I'm relieved she's not coming with me because my mind is reeling, and I need quiet to think. By the time I'm dropped off at Luca's door, I know what I have to do.

I first go to Luca's room and search for my bag. I can't find it and decide I don't need to pack. In fact, it will be easier if I don't. I have plenty of clothes in New York, assuming Niko hasn't tossed them out. The question is can I get home, and will Niko take me in, protect me if needed?

I leave the room, heading downstairs, skulking about until I find Luca's office. Trying the knob, I find it's unlocked. I slip in, shutting the door. If I'm caught, who knows what will happen to me. Luca will probably lock me up. Didn't he tell me it's within his right to force me to stay?

I stop for a moment, remembering he gave me a choice. But did he really? He'd seduced me to manipulate me to make sure I chose him. He's angry at Niko. Would he do something to me to get back at him? God, I'm so confused.

I find a landline phone and pick up the receiver, listening to see if it works. The buzz sound is different in Italy, but it appears to work. Having lived in Europe for years, I know how to call the United States. I dial the country code and then Niko's number.

"Unless you're returning Aria, we have nothing to talk about."

I'm so relieved to hear his voice. "It's me, Niko."

"Aria? Are you okay? What has that fucker done to you?"

"Ah..." Technically, I'm alright. Mostly, I'm embarrassed and feeling like a stupid woman. "I'm fine, but I want to come home."

"He won't let you?"

"I don't know. He's out of town. I just—"

"I can't get a plane there until tomorrow, but I can get you a ticket. Can you get to the airport?"

I have no idea. But I'd escaped his place. I'll find a way out of Luca's. "I'll find a way."

"Where's your phone?" Niko knows Luca would have taken my phone.

"I don't have it. Hold on." I start opening drawers in Luca's desk. It's a fool's quest except there in the bottom drawer is my phone. "I found it, but I don't know if it works." I turn the phone on. I'm down to thirty percent battery life. "I don't know if the SIM card is in it."

"That's okay." He rattles off apps not requiring a SIM card that I can use to contact him. "Keep the phone with you, but hide it, okay? I'll send you flight details when I have them."

"Okay." The line is quiet for long moments. "I'm sorry—"

"Just come home, Aria. Be careful. Be smart. And come home."

I hang up, shoving the phone inside my dress's bodice. I sneak out of Luca's office and head back to my room to change. I put on jeans and a T-shirt with a sweater over it. I slip on a pair of ankle boots and shove the phone inside. It's uncomfortable to walk, but I make my way down to the kitchen.

"I miss Luca," I announce. "I'm supposed to be with him."

The young servant looks at me with a lost expression. "*Mi dispiaci, no capito.*" She doesn't understand.

"*Luca. Io voglio Luca. Auto?*" I tell her I want Luca and improvise driving with my hands to see if I can get a car.

She bites her lip, then says something in Italian. Her eyes glance toward a small cupboard near the back door. I go to it, opening it to find several sets of keys. I pick the one that I'm sure isn't a sports car and head out back.

"*Io vado a Luca a Roma.*" I'm going to Luca in Rome, I tell her.

She still looks uncertain but doesn't stop me.

"It's a surprise," I tell her. "*Surpriso?*"

She tilts her head. "*Sorpresa?*"

I nod. "Yes." I press my index finger over my mouth hoping that "shh" is a universal sign. I don't want her to call him or tell anyone.

She nods, and I exit the kitchen into a breezeway that leads to the garage. I find the car, happy that it's a sedan, and climb in. If I can get out the gate, I'm as good as gone.

I pull the car out and head toward the gate. I don't know where the airport is, but I plan to wait to set the GPS until I'm away from here. I don't want the guards to see.

As I approach the gate, I'm surprised that it opens. As I slowly drive through, one of Luca's men waves. I'm shocked. I'm also a little worried about what will happen to the guard when Luca realizes this man let me go. But I can't think of that.

Once to the road, I turn right heading to the town using the route Bianca took me. At the first open spot, I pull over and enter the Rome Airport into GPS. The map with the most direct route feels like a lifeline.

I follow it, my hands gripping the wheel. I know I won't be safe until I'm on the plane in the air heading to New York. But the farther I get from Luca's villa, the more I can breathe. Soon, I'll be home and safe with my family.

I have a pang of sadness at leaving, but I remind myself that the feeling is for the Luca I thought he was and for the life I thought we might have. But now I know the truth about him. He's a lethal, manipulative man, and I was a fool to fall for him.

13

LUCA

I sit in the club, watching, waiting. Carmine suspected a group of Americans could be soldiers of Niko's. It doesn't take long for me to determine they're likely employees of the U.S. Embassy located up the street. So, I relax and enjoy my drink. Tonight, once I return to my apartment, I'll call Aria, and I hope to hear her enthused voice tell me about buying a wedding dress. I'm regretting my heavy-handedness with her before I left. My conscience hasn't let me forget the hurt I saw in her eyes.

But I feel like I know her well enough to believe that she'll get past my behavior and return to being the effervescent woman who captivated me from the moment I saw her. I love her energy and how she sees the positive and fun in nearly everything. Being around her lifts me, lights me up, and I don't want to lose that. I definitely don't want to be the cause of her inner glow dimming.

So, I'll call her later and prod her to share her day. I'll let her know the plans so far for the wedding, the vows, the flowers, and the cases of champagne I've had ordered. Maybe I can coax her into phone sex. My dick twitches at the possibility.

My thoughts of Aria are interrupted by Electra sauntering up to my table. She sits, and her hand slides up my thigh, brushing over my dick. It retreats from her touch.

I lift my glass of scotch to my lips. "Remove your hand." I down my drink and prepare to leave.

She defies me, cupping me. "I can still make you happy. Your wife—"

I turn my head to look at her with an expression I normally reserve for my enemies. "I said, remove your hand."

She flinches and jerks her hand back. I see fear for a moment, but then she comports herself. "Have I done something to earn this disdain? Have I not been good to you? Have I not pleasured you well enough?"

I sigh. It's not her fault that Aria has effectively cut off any attraction I once felt for Electra. Or any woman. Electra was a favorite of mine for a time, but she's certainly not the only woman I've fucked.

"I enjoyed our time together, Electra, but now it's over." I rise and button my coat.

"Over?" She stares up at me in confusion. "How will I—"

"You've been well compensated. Your work pays you well, does it not? And you're welcome to find someone new." I glance over and see Gino watching us again. If he's generous with money or gifts, Electra will be happy to service him.

"I don't want someone new. I love—"

"I'm getting married." I see Bruno nod at me, letting me know he needs to talk. "I have to go. *Ciao*, Electra." I leave before she can respond. I head to the back office where he and Carmine are waiting.

"We got a call from Tomaso. Aria took a car and is heading to Rome."

Immediately, my gut clenches and I go on alert. "What?" I pull my phone from my pocket wondering if she called me, then I remember

I took her phone. I planned to give it back to her with a new SIM card on our wedding day. The day she would be mine. So there's no call from her, but I see one from Tomaso.

"He said he tried to call you. He checked with the house, and apparently, she misses you." Bruno smirks.

"She's coming to me?" The tightness in my chest loosens, but not all the way.

"That's what Issa told Roberta."

"And she took a car?" Why didn't she have one of my men drive her?

Bruno is stifling a laugh. "Not the Lamborghini or Maserati, though."

Good. She might kill herself driving those. "Do we have tracking on the car she took?"

"You don't think she's coming here?" Bruno asks.

I don't want him to know my concern that perhaps Aria changed her mind and is exercising the permission I gave her to return home. "I'm worried she'll get lost."

"Oh. Right." He pulls out his phone, presumably to find the location of the car Aria took. A moment later, he says, "She's on the E80 heading south."

I nod. That's how to get to Rome. It's also how to get to the airport. But she wouldn't just leave. I told her I'd let her go if that is her choice. She has no reason to run away from me. Plus, she told Issa she missed me. I'm worrying for nothing.

"Keep an eye on her. I'm heading back to the apartment." I have to get ready for her arrival.

Bruno nods. "What about the Americans?"

"They look like government workers, but keep an eye on them as well." It isn't like I don't have government officials and law enforcement on my payroll. Niko could bribe someone here to spy on me.

As I make my way out of the club, Electra stops me again. "You can't just throw me away."

Irritation flares. "You're trying my patience."

She swallows hard but holds her ground. "I deserve more—"

I lean in, wanting her to see the seriousness in my eyes. "I don't owe you anything. If you're not careful, you'll have less than you have now."

I push past her, nodding to one of my men, who steps in front of her to block her from following me.

As my driver brings me back to my apartment, I arrange for a meal, champagne, and flowers to be delivered. I'm not a romantic man, or at least I haven't been. For the most part, I don't care much about what women think of me or how I treat them.

Not that I go out of my way to be an asshole, but wooing a woman isn't something I've ever done. Not until Aria.

It's a little disconcerting how much effort I've gone through to make her mine. And now, I'm doing things to make sure she doesn't change her mind. The woman has me wrapped around her finger, and I can't deny that I don't like it. No one should have power over me like that. But I know she's the one for me, and so I'm going to do what I have to do to make sure she stays with me.

When I arrive home, I pour a glass of scotch and then go to my room to change into something more casual, hoping it will make me look less like a Mafia Don and more like the man she ran away to be with.

Thirty minutes later, my order arrives. My guesstimate is that Aria will arrive in twenty minutes, so I put the food in the oven. I set the flowers out and put the champagne on ice to keep it cold. Then I wait. That's another new experience, and it too is unsettling. I've waited a lot for Aria. I'll make my apologies to her for my brutish behavior the other night, but I also will make her understand that I've done a great deal against my usual nature for her. She can't question my commitment anymore.

Nearly thirty minutes later, I'm feeling agitated. Is she lost? Does she even know to come here? I'm getting ready to call Bruno, but my phone rings from him first.

"Where is she?" I demand.

"She's at the airport."

My heart drops. She's leaving. I don't like how it feels to know this woman I've put so much time and emotion into is betraying me like this, so I resort to the emotion I can manage best. Anger.

I have two options. Have one of my men who works at airport customs stop her and drag her back to me. Or I can let her go and never think of her again. I don't like either option.

"I've called Arturo to keep an eye on her," Bruno says of my customs agent. "Do you want him to stop her?"

Fuck. I do want him to stop her, but if I do, she'll hate me. Normally, I might not care, but something about Aria makes me need her respect and affection. Plus, I'll kiss my business in the United States goodbye, as Niko will burn everything I have there down. I could fight it, but my holdings there aren't strong enough yet.

She doesn't want me. That realization hits, and again I'm filled with anger that she'd treat me like this. I'm Don Luca Conte. I'm not going to be brought down by a woman.

"No. Let her go. I'm done with her."

14

ARIA

I find a parking spot, not sure what sort of lot it is. Once I'm aboard the flight, I'll message Luca and tell him where the car is. As I exit the car, I'm apprehensive. I've felt this for nearly the entire drive. I keep expecting Luca or one of his men to stop me. So far, no one has, but I'm not free yet.

Along with my apprehension is doubt in my judgment. I shouldn't have been so impulsive to come to Italy. At the same time, am I being impulsive to leave without talking to Luca? He said I had a choice. I could ask him about that woman in the picture.

I pick up the pace to the terminal knowing that Luca has power over me. His gentle way and soft touches seduce me into compliance, manipulate me into accepting situations I wouldn't normally accept. I need to leave now, before we're married. Before the Mafia world sees me as his property.

I'm just about to the road that runs in front of the terminal when a man comes toward me, stumbles, and crashes into me. He knocks me off balance, and I fall to the pavement.

"*Scusa*," he says, reaching down to help me up. He continues talking in Italian that I don't understand.

I open my mouth to tell him it's okay when I feel a pinch in my neck. My hand immediately presses against it as I look at him.

"*Ti rilassi*. Relax."

My world tilts again, but this time it's from the inside, not from being knocked down. I try to pull away, but he holds me, speaking in words I don't understand.

"Luca said I could go." I'm not sure if the words actually make it out of my mouth. My mouth feels like it has cotton in it, unable to form coherent words or scream. Why is Luca doing this? Why this way?

The man tugs me back to the garage. Inside, I'm panicking, but I can't get my body to fight.

We reach a car, and he opens the back door and pushes me in. He then slams the door and climbs in the front seat. There's another man in the driver's seat and they're talking. I grope around, but it's like my brain and my body can't coordinate. A fog is descending on me, and as much as I try to fight it, I can't. Moments later, everything goes dark.

I WAKE. My first sensation is the pounding in my head. I go to press my fingers to my temple, but my hand jerks to a stop from restraints. I open my eyes and find myself on a bed, my hands cuffed to the head-board. The stench in the room nearly makes me vomit.

I tug at my restraints knowing I need to get free. My wrists sting and burn from the effort. I yell out, and the door flies open. I flinch, and instinct has me trying to recoil from the three men entering.

One of the men stands at the end of the bed. He speaks in Italian. I have no clue what he's saying, but the tone and leering tell me it's not good. He grabs my ankles, trying to force my legs apart.

"Stop!" I kick at him, one of my efforts hitting him in the chin.

He jerks back, violence shining in his eyes. He yells at me, slapping me against the face and spitting on me. "*La puttana di Luca.*"

I recognize that word. Whore. He's calling me Luca's whore. So these aren't Luca's men.

He pulls a phone out, continuing to speak in words that aren't likely complementary. Holding his phone at me, he snaps a picture.

"*Andiamo,*" he says to the men, and they all leave.

Once they're gone, I struggle to get free, but it's no use. I give in, sagging into the dirty mattress. I wonder what sort of germs I'm going to catch but then decide whatever is lurking in the mattress is probably less lethal than the men who've kidnapped me.

Why did I come here? Niko is right, I'm immature. I have my head in the clouds. But I'd been so sure Luca loved me, or at least cared about me. Unable to stop the tears, I cry until exhaustion brings on a fitful sleep.

I WAKE, and it takes a moment to orient myself. This isn't a dream. I've been kidnapped and am being held by a man who is likely Luca's enemy and will kill me. I shirk away from him, hoping he doesn't try to touch me again.

"Who are you?" he asks in English.

I consider my answer carefully. Do I say I'm Luca's fiancée? Probably not. That might make things worse for me. Does he know my brother? Would knowing I'm a Leone be helpful or a hindrance?

He waves a gun. "Do you speak English? Who are you?"

"Aria Leone."

He doesn't react, making me think he doesn't know my brother.

"Where are you from? Why are you here?"

"New York." I don't answer the latter question. What can I say? I'm here because I'm naïve and stupid to believe in love and happily ever after.

He tilts his head. "Don Conte brought a plaything home from his visit to New York?"

I want to deny it, but I'm convinced that Luca doesn't see this relationship like I do. I'm either just a toy or a pawn to get back at my brother for something.

"You dance too?" His eyes rake down my body, sending a shiver of fear and disgust through me.

"I'm Don Niko Leone's sister." In hindsight, perhaps I shouldn't have admitted that.

He stares at me for a long moment. Then he shrugs and pulls out his phone. After poking at it, he puts it up to his ear. "How much do you think Don Conte thinks you're worth?"

"It doesn't matter what I'm worth. You take something from a Don, they'll hunt you down and kill you."

He laughs. "And when he does, I'll kill him and take over his Family."

So this man is from a rival Family?

He puts the phone in his pocket. "Don Conte doesn't seem too interested in you anymore. Of course, he has more than one toy." He sighs, scraping his hand over his face in what I suspect is fatigue. "I really thought you'd be more useful to me."

He stands and moves to the edge of the bed. Panic rips through me. Is he going to kill me or assault me? Maybe both.

15

LUCA

I'm drinking another scotch, knowing I shouldn't, but unable to stop myself. I like control, and too much booze robs one of that. But my chest is filled with an ache that I want to get rid of. I'm thinking that no amount of scotch will work.

My phone rings. Seeing it's Bruno, I pick up the line. "*Pronto.*"

"The car is parked in the garage. She was booked on a flight that left ten minutes ago."

"I thought I told you to—"

"I had to find the car. Since I was there, I thought I'd find out what was up." Bruno is nothing if not efficient.

"Get the car back to my villa."

"Of course. The thing is, Boss—"

"I don't want to know—"

"She didn't make the flight."

It takes a moment for the words to get through my scotch-soaked brain. "Where is she?" What is going on? My phone pings with a notification, but I ignore it.

"I don't know. I've been able to look at surveillance inside the airport, but it doesn't appear she made it in."

I wonder what that could mean. "Maybe Niko or someone met her and took her to the private airport."

"Maybe."

There's something about his tone that tells me he's not buying it. "What are you thinking?"

"I'm thinking that if she hasn't been rescued, she's either hiding or missing. If the latter, that could be a problem with Don Leone."

Fucking Niko. He's the last person I want to think about now.

My phone pings again, this time with a call notification. Who the fuck is trying to call me now? I ignore it.

"Get eyes and ears—"

"On it. And I'm working on getting the surveillance from outside the airport."

"Good. Let me know." I hang up and glance at my phone to see if the notifications are important. I recognize Sabini's number. An unsettling feeling grips my gut. There is no voicemail, but I see a text with an image. I click it and my blood boils. That motherfucker has dared to touch what is mine?

I call Bruno back. "It's Sabini." My brain is short circuiting. I can't be sure if it's the booze or the rage that is burning like an inferno inside me. When I get that bastard, I'm going to rip him to shreds, slowly, painfully.

"Aw, fuck. Where?"

"I don't know." The image looks like a dirty room. It could be a hotel. A safehouse.

"We could raid that warehouse. Rumor is he has a shipment of women about to be moved. Maybe she's one of them."

It doesn't seem possible that I can be more pissed than I am, but the thought of Aria being sold to some fucking rapist nearly gives me a coronary. I'm not a good man. I commit many crimes every day. But there are a few business endeavors I'll never do. One is sex trafficking.

I head to the kitchen to make coffee. "Get it organized. I want everyone we can spare on this."

I work to sober up, and an hour later, I pull up to Sabini's warehouse with nearly twenty of my men.

"Kill them all. If you find any women, escort them out to someplace safe and call the authorities. Make sure they can't link us. You're just good Samaritans." I turn my attention to Gino and Leonardo. "If I find out one of you has touched them inappropriately, I'm going to cut off your dick and make you eat it. Got it?"

"Yes, Boss."

"If you find Aria, get her safe and call me."

I want to burst in guns blazing, but I don't want collateral damage if they do have Aria or other women. So, we sneak in, one by one, taking Sabini's men out except for one. Bruno drags him to a chair, tying him down.

"This is Sabini's underboss, Aldo," Paolo says.

The multiple scars on his face, some newer than others, make it look like he's been in scrapes like this before. It means he'll be difficult to break. Difficult, but not impossible.

I grab a chair and sit in front of him.

"You're wasting your time, Don Conte. I won't talk," he says.

I nod. "I understand. But all I want is the woman. It's bad enough that Enzo is bringing me down on you and all your men, but that woman's brother doesn't see the Atlantic Ocean as an obstacle to coming here and burning Rome down. Don Leone? Have you heard of him? I'm sure you have. Enzo has a hard-on to get into the American market."

Aldo shrugs like nothing I'm saying matters.

"That's Leone's sister Enzo has tied to a dirty bed."

Aldo's brow furrows, and I'm guessing that he wasn't aware of who Aria was.

"And if he's fucked her..." The idea of it nearly makes me retch. "Leone will string your dicks up for every made man to see." That's not true. I'll string their dicks up first, but I want Aldo to think he can make a deal with me. "Tell me where she is."

He spits at my feet. "You're killing me anyway."

"That's true. I'm sorry for it. Had you come into my Family instead of Sabini's, I imagine you'd be better respected and appreciated."

He sneers.

"The thing is, Aldo, you might be a dead man, but you still have choices. You can tell me where Aria Leone is being held and die a quick, painless, dignified death, or you can protect Enzo, who you and I both know would squeal like a pig, and die a slow, painful death."

"You don't scare me. I've been cut many times."

Paolo nods, holding up his hand, showing only three fingers indicating that Aldo has lost two.

I'm doing my best to be patient. The truth is, calm terrifies people even more than bloodthirsty rampages. But Aria doesn't have time.

I stand. "Strip him."

My men's brows furrow in confusion, but they obey, using their knives to cut away Aldo's shirt.

"Pants too."

Only then do Aldo's eyes flash with fear. It's only a nanosecond, but I see it. When his pants are cut away, I pull my knife and stand over him.

"You're a tough guy, Aldo. I admire that. I wish you were one of my men. But you made your choice not to help me. So, I'm going to castrate you and choke you with your dick."

My men shift uncomfortably, exchanging glances. It's not that I'm not a violent man. But twice tonight, I've threatened castration, and that is new. I've never done it before. But in both cases, it feels warranted.

"That's how you'll be found, Aldo. Naked, having swallowed your own dick."

He snorts like a bull. I admire his effort to stay strong, but I don't have time for this.

"Normally, I might cut your balls off first, but I'm in a hurry." I toy with his shriveled dick with the tip of my knife. His stomach tightens and he tries to move back. "Where is Aria?"

"Go to hell."

I run the knife along the edge of him. Droplets of blood appear.

Aldo grits his teeth. "You like dick, do you, Conte?"

I lean over and get into his face. "You're the one who'll be eating dick." I poke the tip of my blade into his dick and begin to push. It pierces the skin, descending into his shaft.

"Fuck!" Aldo jerks, his chair jumping back, causing the blade to cut along the length again. He rattles off an address.

I look up at Bruno, who is already researching it on his phone. "Could be Sabini's," he says. "It's an abandoned hotel outside of Rome."

I pull out my gun and hold it to Aldo's head.

"What if he's lying?" Bruno asks.

"If he's lying, he's not going to ever tell me the truth. But I don't have time to fuck around anymore. *Ciao*, Aldo." I pull the trigger and march out of the room.

Moments later, I'm in the car and we're racing to the abandoned hotel.

"What about Don Leone?" Bruno asks.

"What about him?" I ask the question even though I know what he's asking. He's thinking I should contact Niko. I probably should. But right now, my focus is on saving Aria.

It takes longer than I'd like to get to the hotel. When we arrive, we enter like the military, quietly but swiftly. We reach a room that I'm sure is the one Aria was held in the picture. There are ties still on the bed. But she's not here.

"Fuck!"

"He must have heard about the warehouse," Bruno says.

As if on cue, my phone buzzes with another notification. Another picture appears. Aria is on another bed, her eyes are closed, and I'm terrified she's dead.

You think you're smarter than me, Enzo texts.

I nearly hurl my phone in frustration but manage to rein it in. I'm going to store up this rage and take it out on Enzo Sabini.

"Sabini is texting. Who do we know that can help us trace him?"

"Cabella has a guy," Bruno says, already tapping on his phone.

Taking the woman proves otherwise, I text back to Enzo.

I imagine her brother will thank me when he learns I rescued her.

I shake my head, thinking this would be funny if Aria weren't in a bad situation. *If you believe that, then you're too stupid to live.*

I guess we'll see.

I think for a moment on how to respond. I want to kill this man so badly I can taste it. I also want to scare the shit out of him. The question is, will that make him panic and hurt Aria? Or will it unsettle him, as I want?

I'll see you dead, and more likely than not, it will be Don Niko Leone who sends you to hell. I'd wish you luck, but nothing can save you now.

I look at Bruno. "How long before they can track him?"

"Working on it." Not fucking fast enough.

My phone rings. I look, thinking it's Sabini. Maybe he'll work with me, after all. Instead, I see Niko's number.

I want to ignore it but know I can't. He deserves my respect in this situation. "*Pronto.*"

"Where the fuck is my sister? I know she's not on the flight I arranged for her."

"She was taken by Enzo Sabini."

"Who the fuck is that?"

So Enzo hasn't contacted Niko yet. "He's a dead man when I find him. He may tell you that he's saved Aria, but it's not true. He has her tied up." I wonder if I should send him the pictures so he believes me. I don't care if Niko is my enemy. He can be a help to find Aria if I can keep him on my side for now.

"I'm coming to Rome."

I want to tell him to stay off my turf, but I know I can't. I have to remember that Aria made her choice. She wants to go home and clearly found a way to reach Niko, who arranged her return. I have to respect that.

I hang up and turn to Bruno. "Any word?"

Bruno holds up his phone with a map.

"Let's go kill this motherfucker."

16

ARIA

Consciousness breaks through the fog. With it comes overwhelming hopelessness. I don't know how long I've been here. I was moved from the dingy place, and while this place isn't the Ritz, it's cleaner and doesn't smell bad. Not that it matters. Whenever I wake up, someone is back to drug me again, and everything, including my environment, slips away. For that reason, I lie quietly with my eyes closed. As sensation returns to me, I reconsider going back to sleep. I'm hungry and thirsty. My wrists are raw and burning.

The door opens, and I can't help instinctively flinching and tensing as my captor approaches. He pulls a chair next to the bed.

"Wake up!" He pokes at me.

"If you don't want me to sleep, stop drugging me." It occurs to me, once the words are out of my mouth, that I shouldn't be so snarky. This man could kill me at any time. The fact that he hasn't suggests he still thinks I have some value.

"Want to be treated like a princess? I can do that. But you have to do something for me."

I only stare at him.

"Your brother is Don Niko Leone, right?"

I still don't respond.

"You help me form an alliance with him to get rid of Conte and establish myself in New York—"

I laugh even though I know it's not smart. I blame the drugs for lack of control of my responses.

His eyes flare with heat. "You find that funny?"

"Do you know my brother? He won't let you establish yourself in New York."

His jaw tightens. "He was letting Conte—"

"That's a partnership."

"Fine. Partnership."

My brain is starting to clear. "What do you have to offer?"

He's the one laughing this time. "You."

I have no doubt that my brother loves me and will do what he needs to protect me, but he won't go into business with someone who is holding his sister hostage.

"So, your plan is to use me to get my brother to kill Luca and become a partner with you?"

He nods.

"And once I'm released, you think my brother will still want to do business with you?"

"I've saved you from Conte. He'll be grateful."

I rattle my handcuffed arm. "This isn't saving."

"I haven't forced myself on you or let my men touch you. I saved you from that. And you wanted away from Conte, right? I saved you from that."

I decide that if I want to get free, my best bet is to go along. My brother will eventually kill him, but by then I'll be free. Well, probably not free. Once I return to New York, Niko will likely lock me away. Or marry me off to one of his capos. My life won't be much different than it is now except, of course, the restraints won't dig into my wrists.

But if I go along, will Niko really help kill Luca? I imagine he will to save me. I can't be a part of that. Luca didn't turn out to be the man I thought he was, but that doesn't mean he should die. He gave me a choice, and I was the one who impulsively ran off when he said he'd send me home if I wanted. I'm here because of me, not Luca.

"Have you contacted my brother?"

"That's where you come in. You do your part, and everything will be okay. If not..." His eyes rake over my body. "Well, you're a beautiful woman..."

"My brother is *Il Soldato della Morte*. You don't want to make an enemy of him, Don...?" I figure he has to be a Don.

"Sabini, and your brother don't scare me."

Then you're an idiot.

He holds up his phone. "You're to contact him. Let him know you're okay. Tell him to do business with me. If you say anything that turns him against me, I'll kill you."

I swallow and nod.

"Give me his number."

I rattle off Niko's number and can't decide whether I want him to answer or not. He may not pick up the phone since he won't know the number.

"Who is this?" Niko's voice comes through the phone.

"Don Leone, I'm Don Sabini. I have good news for you. I've saved your sister from Don Conte."

There is a pause, and I know my brother is assessing, thinking, planning. He's angry at Luca, but Niko also knows Luca.

"Let me speak to her."

Don Sabini holds out the phone to me as he mouths, "Be careful."

My mind is a whirl trying to come up with a coded way to let him know the situation. Niko is expecting me to be on a plane heading to New York. He must be suspicious about why I've missed it.

"Aria?"

"I'm sorry I missed the flight."

"Are you okay?"

"I'm fine. This place is like when we were kids. Remember how Lorenzo used to play Don?" I bring up a childhood game my brother Lorenzo and Niko would play with me. It's been awhile since Niko and I have talked about our brother, who died along with our mother at the hands of rival Families.

Sabini's eyes narrow at me.

"Treated me like a princess," I finish. Of course, that isn't how it was. I'd be put in a closet, and Lorenzo and Niko would pretend to be looking for me to save me from an enemy Family. In hindsight, it's an odd game for children, but considering the violence in our lives, it makes perfect sense.

"Where are you?" He must know that Sabini is listening as he doesn't give any indication that he understands my message.

"Don Sabini has me."

He takes the phone. "She's in good care."

"I appreciate your saving my sister. I'm on my way to Italy as we speak. Where can I pick her up?"

"I'll give you those details when you arrive. I ask too for a meeting. I've heard much about you, Don Leone. I think we could mutually help each other."

"Is that so?"

"We have a common enemy. Luca Conte."

"Don Sabini, I'm happy to discuss business with you once my sister is safely headed back to New York."

"I'm sure you can understand my position. I'd prefer to talk with you first."

"I'm sure you're not suggesting that you're holding my sister hostage to coerce me into meeting with you?"

Sabini's lip sneers up. "Of course not. When you land, I'll let you know where we can meet. Your sister will be there. You'll see that she's safe."

"You'll hear from me in a few hours."

The line goes dead. Sabini sits back, lost in thought as if he's assessing the call.

"You got what you wanted," I say, hoping it will assure him.

He rises. "For your sake, I hope so." He goes to leave.

"Can't you take off these restraints? I don't look like a woman who's been rescued." I'm sure my hair is a mess, my clothes are disheveled, and my makeup is probably smeared.

"Not until I hear back from your brother."

His phone beeps. *"Pronto,"* he answers. He listens, and almost immediately, his eyes swing to me, filled with anger. He speaks quickly into the phone in Italian and then shoves it into his pocket. He goes to a table and picks up a syringe. My heart sinks.

"I'd kill you now except I need that deal with your brother."

"What's going on?" I shirk away as he prowls over to me. It's a hopeless move.

He doesn't say anything as he presses the needle into my skin. Almost immediately, I feel the effects. My vision blurs. My mind turns to fog. As I drift away, I hear a loud crash. I think there is yelling and gunfire. Or maybe it's a dream. I don't want to sleep, so I fight it.

I lift my head, watching as Sabini hurries to the door. He flings it open and immediately, his head jerks back. But the pull of the drug is too much, and I succumb to the lure of sleep.

"Aria!" It sounds like Luca. Could it be? The voice yells in Italian, and soon, my hands are free. I try to open my eyes, but it's impossible. Arms wrap around me, holding me, and while I should be trying to run away, I sink into them. They feel like safety.

He's barking out orders in Italian as he lifts me and carries me out of the room. "You're safe, *Mio Angelo.*"

Mio Angelo. My angel. It must be Luca.

Everything is askew, a blur. Like I'm in a funhouse. Then I'm sitting in Luca's lap. Movement suggests we're in a car.

"What did he give you?" he asks.

I try to shake my head that I don't know, but my head is heavy.

His hands cup my cheeks. I look into his eyes, so desperate, so afraid. "Don't leave me, Aria." I don't want to, but darkness descends over me, anyway.

Visions come and go. I'm in New York, and a man arrives looking for Lucy. He's handsome, and he looks at me with an intensity that takes my breath away. Luca. He's the son of Lucy's deceased husband. He's different from other Dons. He has a quiet reserve. He's loyal to his father's wishes, which include helping Lucy in a new life. I find that sweet. Most Dons are fueled by power or revenge, my brother included.

But then I'm in Italy, and I'm confused. Luca is different. Or is he? Maybe it's just that the rules have changed. He's in his element. He's the leader. He's claimed his prize. I simply expected something different. I expected romance and didn't think about life in general. Like a business he had to run and the type of man one had to be as a Mafia Don.

I hear yelling again. I recoil, wishing I could wake but unable to. I must be getting more drugs as I feel a prick in my arm. Something is attached there.

Later, I hear apologies and pleading to get well. Sometimes, I feel a kiss on my temple.

It takes time, but finally, I emerge from the darkness. I'm still groggy, but I'm back in the real world, out of the dream state.

Roberta says something in Italian, and moments later, a commotion sounds in my room.

"You fucking stay away from her." Niko's voice fills the room.

"I will not." Luca's voice is defiant, daring Niko to stop him.

My head is heavy as I turn it to look at the two men I love. Two men who clearly want to kill each other.

17

LUCA

Niko has disrespected me in my own home. In front of my staff. I'm well within my right to kill him here and now. But I don't. Only because of Aria. Who the hell knows what she endured. I won't kill her brother in front of her.

"Mind yourself, Don Leone. You're in my home—"

"Fuck you. She's my sister, and I'm taking her home."

"I never said you couldn't take her home." But God, while she's here in my house, I'm going to pull out all the stops to encourage her to stay. My heart nearly stopped when I thought she might be dying. What would be the point of all this without her by my side?

"Look at her, Niko. She's in no condition to travel. Or is this about your ego? Do you really care for her? If you do, let her heal, for God's sake."

His jaw tightens, and he pushes past me.

Roberta is propping Aria up.

"Get the doctor," I tell her in Italian. She nods but first hands Aria a glass of water.

Aria's eyes are glassy, and yet, I see fear in them.

"You're safe," I tell her. I want to lie next to her, hold her, but I don't have a right. She was leaving me, and so, while it goes against my nature, I step back and let Niko comfort her.

"What happened?" Niko sits on the edge of the bed.

"I was taken at the airport." She glances up at me, and I don't know how to respond. I hate that she was leaving, so I can't smile. "His name was Sabini—"

"He's dead. As are all of his men." It's a fucking mess, too. I'm spending a fortune on law enforcement to cover up the violent rampage. My men are whooshing to take over his business and deal with anyone who thinks they can stop me.

The doctor enters, and Niko rises to give him access to check Aria. When he first examined her, he told me she'd been sedated quite a bit and she was dehydrated, but after rest and IV rehydration, she'd recover physically.

"When can she travel?" Niko demands.

The doctor glances at me over his shoulder. He starts to speak Italian, but I stop him. "Don Leone speaks Italian, but Aria does not." Mostly, I don't want him thinking that by speaking Italian, Niko won't understand him in case he says something I wouldn't want Niko to hear. But also, Aria should know what is being said.

"She's weak. She needs food, fluids, and rest. A week."

I arch a brow.

"Actually, she could use two weeks. She'll need to regain her strength."

Roberta returns with a tray of food. She sets it on the table until the doctor is finished with Aria's checkup.

"Will there be lasting effects from the drugs?" I ask.

"Shouldn't be." The doctor stands.

"*Grazie.*" I nod my appreciation to him. He nods back.

In Italian, I ask Roberta to prepare lunch for Niko.

"I'm not hungry," he says.

"Aria needs her rest. I'm showing you great respect you don't deserve by letting you stay in my home after you've disrespected me over and over—"

"When it comes to Aria, I don't give a shit—"

"It's only because of Aria that I'm putting up with it, but there are limits."

His eyes flash with hatred. "Don't you threaten me."

"I'll remind you that you're in my country, in my home. You don't have to like me, but you will respect me and follow my rules, as I did for you in your country." Hell, I put Aria in my guest room instead of my room, although admittedly, that was less out of respect for Niko as it was respect for Aria since she planned to leave. "You'll leave this room now. I want a moment with Aria."

I glance at her because I have threatened Niko. It probably isn't going to endear me to her. But I won't put up with his disrespect. Not in my house. Not in front of my woman.

"Go, Niko. I'm fine," Aria says weakly.

I feel triumphant that she's supporting my request. I watch Niko expectantly.

He glares at me. "When you're recovered, we're leaving here, Aria. I promise." He leaves, and the tension in the room drops by several degrees.

"I'll help her with lunch," I say to Roberta, dismissing her.

Finally, we're alone, and I sit next to Aria on the bed. It's all I can do not to gather her close. But I can't not touch her.

"*Mio Angelo.*" My hand caresses her cheek. She closes her eyes, leaning into me. It's like a gift.

Tears run down her cheeks, and I can't resist. I wrap her in my arms. "I'm so sorry." I kiss her head and wish I could take back everything that brought her pain. I want to ask her why she ran off, but now is not the time to hash out such things.

"How long have I been... asleep?"

"You've been in and out for a few days. You had IV fluids, but mostly, we've let you rest." I think she's shaking, but then I realize it's me. I feel like I'm coming apart, but I need to hold it together for her.

"That man called Niko. I tried to let him know that it was Sabini, not you—"

"I know. It's okay. Niko doesn't like me, but he knows how I feel about you."

She glances up at me, and I see questions in her eyes. I kiss her gently. "You're okay now, Aria."

"Has Niko been here long?"

Is she already thinking of leaving again?

"He arrived the day we found you."

She settles her head against me, and I feel like maybe I have a chance to put all this right. Except I'm not quite sure where I went wrong except, of course, the ultimatum.

"I'm sorry I just left. I didn't think. Niko's right, I'm too immature and impulsive."

"I think you're perfect, *Mio Angelo*."

She looks up at me, and for the first time in too long, I see the woman I fell for the moment I met her. "You do?"

"Yes, why do you think I want to marry you? But I will say that you should recognize that here, as in New York, you need to take greater caution."

She nods. I want to ask her if she's going to stay, but I find I'm too much of a coward.

The door opens and Roberta pokes her head in. "*Scusa, Don Conte.*" In Italian, she tells me the doctor has left a prescription and that Niko wants to talk to me.

I kiss Aria again and then rise. "You need to eat and rest."

Roberta brings the tray of food to Aria, setting it in her lap.

"I'll be back later."

She nods, giving me a wan smile.

I step out of the room and Niko is waiting. Tension radiates off him in waves. "I know you plan to make her stay—"

"Unlike you, Niko, I don't have to kidnap or coerce a woman to make her stay." Okay, so my ultimatum and seduction might be manipulative, but he kidnapped his wife.

"You don't know what you're talking about. My wife—" He stops. "The point is, Conte, she wants to go home. If not for Sabini, she'd be home. You know that."

I cross my arms and study him. "Would you have forged an alliance with him? Killed me for him?"

"I will do anything to protect my sister."

"I would too. But Sabini would be dead before I killed you."

"And yet, you're threatening me in front of my sister."

I sigh. "I understand that tradition doesn't mean anything to American Mafia. Perhaps that's why so many Bosses have lost their power."

"Traditional has nothing to do with this."

"Respect does."

He shakes his head. "You disrespected me by making my sister run away."

I laugh. "She's a grown woman who decided what she wanted. Is that what irks you? She wants me instead of staying with you?"

His jaw tightens. "What irks me is your taking advantage of her."

I tense and straighten. "I've done no such thing. Yesterday would have been our wedding day."

His eyes widen in surprise but then narrow. "No. Because she decided to come home. I'm staying until I can do that. Now, I'm going to talk to my sister."

He pushes past me, and I want to stop him. I'd like to punch him and toss him out of my home. But for Aria's sake, I don't.

As the door shuts behind him, I pray to my parents' God that Aria will stand strong against her brother. That she'll let me make amends to her and decide to stay with me. That she'll marry me and give my life purpose.

18

ARIA

My stomach is ravenous, but after a few bites of soup and bread, it's also revolting after going so long without food. I push the tray away just as my door opens and Niko walks in.

"*Lasciaci*. Leave us," he says to Roberta.

She turns to me, and I'm struck that she seems to be looking at me for her next order instead of listening to my brother. I've never been in this situation before.

I nod. "*Va bene*," I say to let her know it's okay.

"*Mangia*," she says with a last glance to me before leaving the room.

Niko pulls a chair over and sits. "She's right. You need to eat.

"I am... I just... my stomach needs me to eat slowly."

Silence follows, growing between us. There's emotion radiating off him.

"You could have died." His voice is tight.

"I could say that about you all the time."

"It's not the same." He lets out a frustrated growl. "I don't care what Luca says. As soon as you have your strength back, you're coming home."

I look down at my food. I'm not so sure I want to leave, but saying so will only prove his belief that I'm immature and don't know what I want. Even if he's right, I still should be able to make my own decisions. Although, he'd argue that my last decision nearly got me killed.

"I can't talk about this now." I set the tray aside.

"There's nothing to talk about, anyway. I'll make the arrangements, but you're strong, Aria. We'll leave in two days, three max." He stands. "Keep it to yourself, though. I don't want more hassle from Luca."

I frown. "That's it? You're going to order me around?"

He puts his hands on his hips. "You don't want to stay, do you? Not after everything that's happened."

"You do know that Lou held a gun on me, Elena, and Lucy, right? It's not like scary shit hasn't happened to me around you."

He shakes his head. "Look, you don't feel well. When you're better—"

"When I'm better, what? You'll send me home and lock me away? Or maybe you'll send me to some remote place in France or England. If you're going to lock me up, I'd much rather that."

"What is wrong with you? Did you get hit on the head?"

"So now having an opinion on my own life is the result of a head injury? Do you know how insulting that is?"

He stares at me like I've gone mad.

"What do you care, anyway?"

He gapes. "I beg your pardon. I've done nothing but look out for you since you were ten."

"Right. Look out for me. You shipped me off the first chance you got. First to boarding school, then college. Then—"

"You had a good life."

I nod. "Oh, sure. Money. Fun. But no friends. No family." I shake my head. "If I hadn't come home, I'd have never known you were married. Not known about the twins."

At first he looks like he's going to deny it. "That was an unusual situation."

"Your life—this life—is an unusual situation. One where you ship me off for my quote-unquote safety. But really, it gets me out of your hair. You should have been happy that I left. You can live your life and not think of me... deal with me."

He sighs and sits down. "That's not true, Aria. I love you."

"How would I know that?"

He takes my hand. "I'm sorry you feel abandoned. That wasn't my intention. When you get home, I'll do better. I promise."

I pull my hand away. "You don't need to wait for me."

"Of course I'll wait."

I turn over in bed, away from him. "I don't want you to."

"So, you want to stay here? With the man you not so long ago begged me to get you away from?"

"I don't know what I want, but I do know that I don't want you bossing me around. I don't want you making decisions for me that are simply convenient for you and your happy little family. Go away." I'm so tired. I want to go back to that netherworld where I drift in oblivion.

"I'll send for you when you're feeling better. We can discuss your future when you're home."

I ignore him. When the door closes, I relax and will the darkness to come. Moments later, the door opens again.

"Go away, Niko."

"It's Luca." A moment later, he's lying behind me, spooning his body around mine. "Rest, *Mio Angelo.*"

I settle against him and give in to sleep.

NIKO LEFT. That's what I learn later that night when I wake, still in Luca's arms. I want to keep emotional distance from Luca, but it's not easy. When I first got here, I barely saw the man. Now I can't do anything without him hovering like I'm fragile glass. It's annoying, and yet at the same time, sweet.

When I sleep, Luca works, apparently in a room next door with a monitor so he knows when I wake. Except at night, when he comes into my room and holds me. Our quiet night time conversations remind me of the times we spent in New York. Of the letters we secretly exchanged. But I understand now that while this is one side of Luca, he has many facets, and I can't let myself start dreaming of a fairy tale.

For the next few days, I rest and slowly get stronger.

Three days after Niko leaves, it's the evening and I'm sitting in the window seat reading before bed.

Roberta enters my room, handing me a phone. "Lucia," she says.

"Lucy?" I take the phone, excited to talk to her. "Hello."

"Aria? It's Lucia. Are you okay?"

"Yes. Getting better every day."

"You're on speakerphone. Elena and Kate are here too."

"Hello, Aria," Elena and Kate say.

Tears form. Happy tears at hearing their voices. For a moment, I think I should have had Niko wait and take me home. While I'm not eager to have him boss me around, I do miss my friends.

"Are you mad at me?" I ask.

"Hell no," Lucia says. "But we are worried. Niko seems to think you might be brainwashed or something by Luca."

I roll my eyes. "I'm not brainwashed."

"Is it love?" Elena asks. "Love can brainwash you sometimes."

"My thinking was wonky about Liam for sure."

I smile, missing them more, and happy that they understand. "I guess it is. Which isn't to say that I'll be here forever. I just... Niko won't let me make decisions—"

"And Luca will?"

"Yes." He had said he would before. Over the last few days, he didn't do anything to suggest that he would force me to stay. He didn't talk about the wedding or a future together. At the same time, the way he looked at me, held me, suggested that he wanted me to stay.

"Luca is a good man." Lucia's comment is more to Elena and Kate, I think. To eliminate their concerns. "But if you want to come home, I'll arrange it. Not Niko. And you can stay with me and Donovan."

"Aria, do you really feel Niko abandoned you?" Elena asks gently.

I choose my words carefully. "He was there financially and if I needed protection, but not emotionally. He never told me he was getting married or having kids. I still wouldn't know about it if I hadn't shown up. I know he loves me, but he doesn't want me around."

"That's not true, Ari." Elena is forceful in her statement. "You have to remember, he was young when you lost your mother and brother. He may have wanted you out of the way so he didn't have to worry about you while he... worked."

Anger brews. "You mean exact revenge? For fifteen years?"

"I'm not saying what he did was right, but it came from a good place."

I shrug her words off even though she can't see me. "Well, I'm safe, if that's your concern. I'm going to figure things out here."

"Just remember, you can come home," Lucy said. "We have lots of room at our place."

When the call ends, I go to hand the phone back to Roberta. She shakes her head. "Yours."

I arch a brow. "Are you learning English?"

She gives me a small smile. "A little."

I look at the phone. "Does Luca know?"

The door opens. "Do I know what?" Luca walks in.

I hold up the phone. "She said I could keep the phone."

His smile is soft, hopeful. "I'd planned to give it to you on our... well... I'd planned to return it." He nods to Roberta, who takes it as a signal to leave.

"It's getting late. Are you tired?" he asks.

I nod. "I'll be back." I go to the bathroom, changing into pajamas and doing my nighttime routine, skincare and brushing my teeth.

When I return, he's lying in the bed. He hasn't asked me to move into his room, but he's here with me every night. I'm confused by our arrangement. I feel that he wants me, and yet, there's so much I don't know.

I slip into bed, savoring the feel of him as he spoons his body around mine.

"Why did you invite me here?"

"You know why."

I turn over, looking at him. "I don't know. You could be using me to gain an advantage with Niko, or to get back at him."

His expression is pained as he pushes my hair back, hooking it over my ear. "No, *Mio Angelo*. It's always been you. I tried to do it the right way, asking Niko for permission to marry you, but he said no."

I frown. I know Luca said something about this before, but what is Niko's problem with Luca? It doesn't make sense.

"I left, but I knew I'd never be able to let you go, so I arranged the notes. And you came to me."

I smile. Those times were filled with dreams. But real life is different. More complicated. Messy.

"But you wanted to marry because of Niko's—"

"No. I wanted to marry you always. The hurry to get it done was because of Niko." He sighs. "But you don't want me, and I'll still honor my agreement to let you go."

I look into his dark eyes, seeing the Luca I fell in love with. "What about Electra?"

He jerks back. "What? How do you know about her?"

His question makes me think he wanted to keep her a secret. "There's a picture of you two. When I asked about it, I was told she's your mistress."

"Oh, *Mio Angelo*. Is that why you left?"

I nod.

He gives me a soft laugh. "I won't deny that I've had relations with her, but she's not my mistress. Not since I met you."

"But all the other wives say their husbands have them."

He looks at me with amusement. "I'm not like them. I have thought of no woman since I met you, haven't slept with a woman since I met you. You've captured my soul."

Can I believe him? I have to if I want a love anywhere close to what my brother has with Elena. Or Lucy has with Donovan. I think of Kate, who took the biggest risk of all in loving Liam. Could I do the same?

I look down as all my thoughts scramble for attention. His finger hooks under my chin and lifts my head to look at him.

"I hope you'll stay. And if you do, I ask that you talk to me when you have questions. I won't lie to you, Aria. That I promise."

I nod, wanting more than anything for him to be speaking the truth.

"Is there more that concerns you?"

"My brother is a pain in the ass, but he's my only family. Blood family, anyway. I don't want to have to choose."

He sucks in a breath. "I will not be the one who makes you choose, but I can't say what he will do. And... I don't think I can ever go to New York. After what just happened, it will be difficult for me to let you go anywhere without me."

There is some machismo in his answer, and yet, I can also see the sincere concern for me in his eyes. It's not just his ego at stake if something happens to me by a rival Family.

"I understand it will be difficult. We'll have to figure something out."

His fingers brush along my cheek. "Does this mean you're going to stay? At least for now?"

"At least for now." My gaze drifts to his lips, and I'm filled with a need to have him kiss me. "In America, this is where we kiss and make up."

He smiles. "Just kiss?"

"Kiss me, and we'll see what happens."

His lips are soft and gentle on mine. Then he tugs me close and holds me. I get the feeling he's not planning to do more.

I push him back and straddle him.

He arches a brow as he looks up at me. "What are you doing?"

"Kissing and making up." I lean over and kiss him. I turn up the heat on it until he groans.

"You're not fully rested—"

"I'm rested enough. I want you. Are you going to help me or do I need to do it myself?"

Heat flashes in his eyes. "I'd like to see you pleasure yourself, *Mio Angelo*."

Okay, so that would be embarrassing. "I meant I'd take control and use your body."

He laughs. "I'd like that too."

I fumble at his clothes until he's naked. It's not easy because he's tugging at my clothes, and then sucking, touching me as my skin is exposed. It's distracting. But finally, I'm straddled over him, rubbing my hands over his broad chest and lower. Feeling his muscles tighten as my fingers brush down. Watching as his dick twitches of its own accord.

"Will you tell me what to do?" I'm a little self-conscious about my lack of experience, but I trust Luca to not laugh or make me feel embarrassed.

He sits up, his fingers running along my neck to the nape and then threading into my hair. "There is no need to teach. Pleasures of the flesh are all about doing what feels good. What do you want to do?"

I rub my pussy over his dick. He lets out a small growl. "See, you know what to do." He kisses me, his lips trailing down until he licks my nipple.

"Oh!" I rock, his dick sliding over my clit. But I want more. Need more. I rise over him. "Luca."

"*Si, Mio Angelo.*" His hand settles on my hip, guiding me until I feel his velvety tip at my pussy. I lower down, taking him inside me. He fills me, expands inside me. It's so deliciously sensual. His face buries along my neck. "So good, *Mio Angelo*. Yes?"

"Yes," I agree as I slide up and then down again. I close my eyes, savoring the flood of fire and electricity coursing through my body.

He lies back, and I do it again, up, down, forward, back.

"You're so beautiful."

His words fill me in another way. Emotion blooms in my chest.

"Ride me, Aria. Make me come." His hands slide up and down my thighs and then up my belly to my breasts. He pinches my nipples. I cry out at the shock of arousal that shoots to my pussy.

"Oh, God, Luca." I lean forward, resting my hand on his chest to gain purchase. My hips move to a rhythm my desire sets. Faster, harder... I'm gasping for breath.

"Yes... right there." He arches, sliding deeper still.

I feel wild, careening out of control to the edge until I'm there. I rock, and his body pulses inside me, hitting a spot that sends me flying.

"Oh, fuck... Yes, Aria." He lets out a long, feral moan. His dick is so hard, I can feel the ridges of him. It makes me come again, or maybe it's the same orgasm. I don't know. All I know is that it's so, so good. Even when my muscles give out and I collapse over him, my pussy pulses. His dick throbs.

His arms wrap around me, hold me like he'll never let me go. And I don't want him to. Not ever.

19

LUCA

I haven't secured my relationship with Aria yet, but I'm feeling more positive about the ability to do so. There is much work to be done in my business, but it has to wait as I lie next to Aria and she falls asleep in my arms.

From a business perspective, I can't afford to spend so much time away. Not if I don't want anyone to take advantage of my current vulnerability. I don't only have my own business to run, but I need to take over Sabini's, so my and my men's time is spread thin. But any losses I might incur in business, I can recapture. That may not be true with Aria. I'm already on my second, maybe third chance with her. I don't imagine I'll have any more. So, I settle in for the night next to the woman I love.

I wake up early, and with a soft kiss to Aria's temple, I slide out of bed and prepare for the day.

Down at breakfast, I'm reviewing all the tasks on my list as I drink my espresso. Roberta enters the dining room with a young woman I know to be her daughter.

"Don Conte. You remember my daughter Lia?"

I nod. "How are you, Lia?" If I remember correctly, Lia should be finishing school this year and either heading off to university or to a job.

"She's back to work this summer," Roberta informs me.

Yes, now I remember. For the last two years, she's come to work alongside Roberta. "Welcome back."

"*Grazia, Don Conte,*" Lia replies.

A thought comes to me. "You speak English, don't you, Lia?"

She glances at her mother with uncertainty in her expression. Roberta nods to her to respond. When she turns back to me, Lia says, "I learned English in school, but I don't know how well I speak it."

"Would you like to improve it? I would love it if you could be available to Aria. You can help her learn Italian, and she can help you with English. I'd like somebody here who can speak English when I'm not available to translate." I pause for a moment and add, "I'm willing to compensate you for the extra time and the expertise."

This time, when Lia glances at her mother, her eyes are wide, and I can see that this is good news for her.

"*Grazia, Don Conte.* I would be happy to perform this work."

With that settled, I finish my coffee and notes for the day. I'm able to work from home today, which will keep me close to Aria if she needs me. Not wanting her to get bored, I send a text to Bianca inviting her over. Moments later, she responds that she and a few of the other wives will be over for lunch.

When I finish breakfast, I return upstairs to the guest room. Aria is sleeping peacefully. I want to climb back in bed and hold her for the rest of the day. Hell, for the rest of my life.

I sit on the edge of the bed, my hand gently caressing along her hip. She stirs and stretches, a smile appearing on her face.

"Are you dreaming about me, *Mio Angelo?*"

"Maybe. But the real thing is better." She wraps her fingers around my tie and tugs me down until our lips press together. In an instant, the rest of the world flies away, and all that exists is Aria. I'm about ready to give in to her when there's a knock on the door. I sit up, telling whoever it is to enter. Roberta, along with Lia, enters the room carrying a breakfast tray.

"Set it on the table," I tell her. Then I turn to Aria. "I'm sorry that I need to be focused on work today. But I want to introduce you to Lia. She's Roberta's daughter. She speaks English, and she'll be able to help communicate when I can't. She's also agreed to help you improve your Italian."

Aria smiles warmly at Lia, and it reminds me why I think she'll be the perfect wife. She's kind even to those whom others with her status might look down on or take for granted.

"*Bongiorno.*"

Lia smiles back. " *Buongiorno, Signorina.*"

"You can call me Aria."

I'm not sure I approve of that. The name everyone should call her is Signora Conte. All in good time, I tell myself.

I take Aria's hand. "You can take all the time you want in bed. You're still supposed to be resting. But Bianca and some of the wives will be up for lunch, unless you want me to cancel."

Aria appears to think about it for a moment but then says, "No, I'd like to see them. All this resting is boring."

I lean over and give her a quick kiss. "I'll be in my office if there's anything important you need." I want her to know that I'm available for her.

"I'll be fine."

Deciding that Aria is well-settled, I head down to my office where Bruno is already waiting.

"Capos are on their way," he reports, sitting with a cup of espresso and checking his phone.

"Good. How's the Sabini cleanup?"

"Pretty much done. The police reported that Sabini's business imploded from the inside out. An attempted takeover from within that caused an internal war."

"Good. What about his business?"

"We've moved in without much resistance. We handed the trafficking victims to the cops."

Along with a few extra bribes, one of the other perks I handed to the police was credit for bringing down Sabini's sex trafficking scheme. It not only makes them look good, but it also protects me. No one will believe that honorable police who free kidnapped women are going to be corrupt. It's a win-win.

Once all my capos arrive, we get to work. Some of the work is tedious, and some of it is annoying, especially when it's clear that Gino is posturing for more control in the business. He's asked to oversee all of Sabini's clubs. That's not happening. Clubs are ideal for money laundering, but also an easy place to skim. I won't give him a chance to steal from me. It's for his own good. I'd have to kill him if he stole, and I don't want to have to do that since my father liked him.

"Everything all right with your new plaything?" Gino asks when we break for lunch.

All the chatter in the room stops, and they know what Gino either doesn't know or care that he's inching over the line. I'm thinking he's posturing to create strife within the organization. If he rattles me or makes me look inept, my men might cross over to him.

I think back to Aria asking me about Electra. She said she saw a picture of Electra with me. It doesn't take much for me to put two and two together. Gino was at the club that night, and he must've sent a picture to Bianca. Bianca is too smart to share it with Aria, but I don't doubt that she shared it with the other wives. That must be how she saw it.

I am calm as I lean back in my chair, lacing my fingers over my belly as I look at him. Outside, I might seem cool as a cucumber, but inside, lethal rage is building. The way my men watch, they know it.

"I made a vow to my father to keep you in the Family, Gino, but you're precariously close to forcing me to break that vow. If I hear you speak Aria's name, or talk about her one more time, I will kill you."

Gino's eyes narrow, but he wisely shuts his mouth.

Deciding I need a moment, I rise from my desk. "Please excuse me. I'll be back in a moment."

I leave my office thinking I'll get some fresh air. It gets pretty stuffy in my office with a bunch of old men, some of whom stick to the old-fashioned ways of bathing, showering only twice a week. Luckily, my generation and younger like a daily shower.

I hear laughter from my mother's sitting room, and I make my way over to it. Aria sits with the wives, enjoying food and drinks, friend-ship and laughter. At seeing her, the tension inside me lessens. She looks relaxed and happy, sitting with a young child in her lap. It strikes me that she belongs here. This is her place. This is now Aria's sitting room.

I watch her, mesmerized as she bounces the toddler and makes cooing sounds to him. In response, he giggles with delight. Emotion wells in my chest as I imagine the child being ours. One of many we'll make to fill this home with life and love.

Aria glances toward me, smiling. It's one of the brightest smiles I've seen from her. Certainly, in a long time.

I smile back and hope that in my expression she can see everything that I want for us and our future.

Reluctantly, I return to my office. I push my men through all the things that need to be done to keep my business thriving and fold Sabini's business into mine.

By the time I dismiss my men, it's late in the afternoon. I sit back in my chair, tilting my head back and closing my eyes.

A soft knock comes to the door. I call out for whoever it is to enter. The door pops open and Aria's head peeks in. I smile because seeing her immediately lights me up.

She walks in, and as she gets closer, her smile wavers. "Is everything all right?"

I nod as I stand and walk to her, pulling her in for a hug. I inhale her scent, gathering strength from her.

She tilts her head back to look at me. "You look tired."

There's no denying it. "I am."

Her fingers trace along my face, and the look she gives me does more to wash away the fatigue than any nap could. "Maybe you should go lie down."

I turn her, maneuvering her back until she's against my desk. "I have a better idea."

She bites her lower lip and her eyes shine with excitement. *Mio Dio*, I love this woman.

"*Ho fame.*" I know she's learned enough Italian to know that I've told her I'm hungry. I slide my hands up her legs, lifting her dress until it bunches at her waist. I tug her panties down, inhaling the sexy, sweet scent of her pussy, already wet and waiting for me.

I lower to my knees, pushing her thighs apart. My mouth waters as I take in her glistening pussy lips. I lean in and drag my tongue through her folds, swirling it around her clit.

"Luca," she says on a gasp, her hand holding my head to her. I drink her in. Lap her up. I drown in her essence until she cries out my name and her juices flow over my tongue. I'm hard as steel. My cock is throbbing, ready to blow.

I undo my belt and pants, shoving them down, needing to get inside her sweet pussy. I step between her legs, ready to sink into her.

"I want my mouth on you again," she says.

Fucking hell. "I'm ready to come." I press forward again, but she puts her hand on my chest and slides off the desk.

"I want to taste you again."

I'm about to explode.

"Did I not do it right last time?"

Her words help me rein in my need. I cup her chin with my hand. "You do it right every time."

"Is there something else you like?"

I have all sorts of fantasies. Deciding my blue balls take a back seat to her need to feel like she can please me, I say, "Take off the top of your dress and your bra."

She looks at me with questioning eyes but does as I ask.

"*Tuo seni sono belli.* Your breasts are beautiful." I fondle one and gently squeeze the rosy hard tip. I want to suck it, but I hold off.

She reaches for my dick. I take her wrist in my hand.

"You can suck, but I want to come on you then lick it off. Are you okay with that?"

She nods. I rub my cock over her lips. My plan is to ease in, but she has other ideas. She sucks my tip hard and then slides her mouth over my shaft. My eyes nearly roll back into my head.

"*Si, Mio Angelo.*" Fuck, her mouth is hot. Watching my cock slide in and out of it is better than any wet dream or fantasy I've ever had. My balls tighten. The end is rushing fast. Too fast. I let out a stream of Italian expletives that I'm not sure Aria knows but will likely guess.

I pull out of her mouth, gripping my dick tight to choke the orgasm about to explode. "I'm going to come now... on you..." I can't stand it. I stroke once, twice, and my cum shoots out, landing on her tits, her chest, her chin. She watches in what looks like fascination. I continue to jerk my cock until my knees buckle.

I drop down in front of her. "You make me come so hard." I want her to know for sure that being with her is not like anything else. Anyone else.

She smiles as she rubs her fingers over my cum. I take her hand, sucking her fingers into my mouth.

"I could do this all night," I say.

"Can we?"

I laugh. "Whatever you want, Aria. I will give it if I can." And I mean it. I'll give her the moon and the stars even if I have to steal them from the heavens.

20

ARIA

Over the next several days, I feel happier than I've ever felt. This is the life I'd expected when I first ran away to be with Luca. When he's with me, he's fully present, showering me with affection, never demanding or giving me ultimatums.

But I like to think I'm a little wiser now. While life feels perfect, I understand that complications and messiness are part of it as well. I acknowledge that I'm in a honeymoon phase and that real life will likely bring occasional conflict.

But I'm feeling hopeful that my future is here with Luca. We haven't talked about marriage again, but I don't see that as a sign of doom like I might have a week ago. There is no hurry, and I believe that over time, if and when we get married, by then, Niko will have calmed down and he, along with the rest of my Family, will be able to attend.

I wake this morning with Luca sitting on the edge of the bed like he has the last several mornings.

"Did you sleep well?" His hand caresses my thigh.

"Yes."

"I have to go out today for work."

"Is everything alright?"

He smiles. "Fine. Sometimes, a king needs to survey his kingdom."

While I'm not aware of anything specific being wrong, I'm sure there are concerns with Sabini's death that need to be addressed. But since my return, Luca always has a gentle, kind composure around me.

"This came." He hands me an envelope.

"What is this?" I sit up in bed and open the back flap.

"There's a baby shower for Lucia that they want to invite you to in New York."

My gaze immediately jerks up to his. "You read my mail?"

For a brief moment, there's a pained expression in his eyes. He shakes his head. "She called me to let me know that it was coming. I believe she was concerned that I wouldn't give it to you."

There's a tension in his voice, but I'm not sure if it's because of my knee-jerk accusation or his concern about whether I'll want to go.

"I'm sorry I—"

"I am late for my meeting, but we can talk about this when I get back."

My eyes narrow. I want to tell him that we don't need a discussion. I can go with or without his permission. But he leans over and gives me a kiss and is out the door before I can express my opinion.

With a sigh, I look at the invitation. I miss my friends, and I really want to celebrate this moment with them. But if I go, will Niko make it difficult to come back? It doesn't matter, I decide. I got to Italy once. I can do it again.

As I shower and dress, I run through my head all the things I want to say to Luca and reasons he should let me go to the baby shower. But then I realize I'm wasting a lot of energy without really knowing what Luca's thoughts are on the situation. So, I push it away and go down for breakfast, where Lia is already waiting for me.

During the morning, I speak Italian, or at least I try with Lia's tutelage and support. Later in the day, we switch, and she speaks English with my support. At any time, if I need to talk to the staff, Lia translates anything I can't get across or understand. This arrangement has been working, and I feel like my Italian is growing stronger.

That afternoon, I head upstairs planning to send a group text to Niko, Elena, Lucy, and Kate about the shower. Group texts are the best way for me to communicate with Niko since the other ladies, or more specifically, Lucy, will keep his attitude in check when he responds to me. Afterward, I plan to take a nap.

I enter Luca's bedroom, where I've moved back into since I decided to stay. I step in the room, and I stop short when I see my closet doors are open. It's not a laundry day, so why would someone be in my closet?

"*Scusa?*"

I hear a bit of a scuffle and then an unknown woman steps out. I don't recall being told about new staff.

"Who are you?" I ask in Italian.

She lifts her chin, looking down her nose at me. Recognition slams into me. This is the woman in the photo Bianca showed me. Luca's former mistress, Electra.

She presses her hand over her stomach, and I see a small swell. My gaze returns to her face. "What are you doing here?" I ask in English as my Italian seems to have vanished.

"You must be Luca's new woman. Has he finally tossed you aside? I see you're not married. But of course, he wouldn't marry you. After all, he's going to be a father."

All the blood drains from my brain, making me lightheaded. I scan the recesses of my mind thinking of anything Luca has said or done to make sense of this woman standing in his bedroom.

"Roberta. Lia. Come here quickly," I yell out the door, hoping they're close enough to hear me.

A moment later, Roberta hurries into the room, stopping short when she sees Electra. "*Oh, mio Dio.*"

Lia follows her in, also skidding to a halt. "*Oh, mama mia.*"

I look at the women. "How did she get in here?"

They glance at each other and then back at me with a shrug.

"We don't know," Lia says.

Electra arches a brow. "You don't think I can get into Luca's home? The father of my child?"

Lia says something to her mother, which I suspect is a translation of what Electra has just said.

Roberta starts rattling off words in Italian faster than I can understand and hurries out of the room.

"My mama is going to get one of the men. They will escort her off the property."

Noting that Electra speaks English, I say, "You need to leave now or you'll be forcibly removed."

Electra's nostrils flare in indignation. She starts speaking in Italian, and while I don't know what she's saying, I imagine it's not complementary.

She strides to the exit. "*Puttana,*" she spits as she passes me.

I'm shaken to the core. Lia puts an arm around me and guides me to the bed. My instinct is to pack and run.

I look up at Lia. "I can't stay—"

"She is not a good woman, Signorina Aria. Don Conte doesn't like her. I promise you."

Roberta returns again, her speech too quick for me to comprehend. Lia responds, I suspect telling her that I want to leave.

Roberta looks at me with concern and says something to Lia.

"My mama says just like I told you. Don Conte doesn't like her."

I want to believe it, but is it that part of me that believes in fairytales? Is it wishful thinking?

Lia nods. "We will call Don Conte. He will tell you."

I shake my head because I can't talk to him. I'm too easily swayed and seduced by him. At the same time, I recognize now, like I hadn't before, that running away isn't the answer, either. Luca told me Electra is in his past, and I believe him. Finding her in my room could suggest that he lied to me, but to what end? Why keep me here if his plan is to be with Electra?

"I will talk to Luca when he gets home this evening. In the meantime, can you call Bianca and invite her over?" If anybody can tell me what is really going on, it will be her.

Twenty minutes later, I'm back in the sitting room as Bianca sweeps in. "Oh *Dio*, did she really come here?"

I work to be strong, but I'm not sure I hide the tremble in my lip. "She got into the house. Into his room. *My* room."

Bianca lets off a string of words in Italian that I suspect would make a sailor blush. "Where is Don Conte?"

"He's working. Somewhere outside of the villa."

She sits next to me on the couch and takes my hand in both of hers, her expression intent on me. "Don Conte does not love this woman. She was his plaything, but he's been done with her for a long time."

I study her. "That picture that came out last week made it seem like it wasn't over. You even said all your men have—"

"Not Don Conte. I saw him when we were here the other day. The way he looks at you. Electra is nothing." She makes a spitting noise.

"She says she's pregnant with his child." Is that even possible? He said they were over for a long time. What is a long time? Weeks? Months?

"It doesn't matter. Electra is a crazy one. At one point, she thought Luca and his stepmother, Lucia—you know her, right?"

I nod. "Her sister is married to my brother."

"She thought Luca and Lucia were together. But it was crazy talk. She was devoted to Giuseppe, and he was to her, even if it wasn't a traditional marriage. And of course, Luca was worried about Lucia when she went to New York."

"She is a fierce woman who can take care of herself."

"I'm sure that is true, but Luca is loyal to his father. He made a vow to him to look out for her." Bianca's brows grow together as if she's considering something. "You know, she was a dancer for him, but the first time he came back from New York, he promoted her. Put her in charge of all the dancers. I bet he did that to compensate for ending things with her. And that's when you met him, is that right? When he was in New York?"

I can see the tale that she's trying to weave, and my heart desperately wants to believe it. Luca ended things with her after meeting me. Didn't he say something like that to me already?

"What if the baby is his?" I ask.

Bianca waves her hand like she's flicking away a tiresome fly. "How do we even know she really is pregnant? She'd do anything to get Luca."

I think about walking into my room and finding her there combined with Bianca's comment about Electra doing anything to get Luca. How far is anything?

"Do you think I'm in danger from her?"

"Nobody would be dumb enough to take something from Don Conte." But Bianca's expression belies the certainty of her statement.

I know that Luca has enemies all around. I'd just spent a harrowing two days with one. But this enemy could be carrying his child and has the ability to get into the house unnoticed. How far will Electra go to get rid of me so she can have Luca?

21

LUCA

I'm sitting in a meeting with Bruno and Stefano, who I'd put in charge of managing Sabini's clubs. At the moment, we are in the back room of one of the clubs that is so seedy I think I'm going to have to take a shower when I get home. The good news is that with a little investment, I think we can turn this place into a nicer establishment.

Stefano is explaining that all the staff in this and the other clubs understand that I'm in charge now and are on board to work with us.

"In fact, they're quite eager for new management," Stefano says.

"Good. What about those who aren't on board?" A few of Sabini's men have tried to come after mine. They seem to be fighting each other more than me to take over Sabini's business. But they did nearly kill one of my men, and I won't have that sort of chaos around. Not now with Aria here.

"We're on it," Bruno says.

I don't need the details as I trust him. My phone vibrates in my pocket, and I take it out to check if it's Aria.

The name of the head of my home security pops up on the screen. "Excuse me for a moment. I need to take this." I rise, fighting the kernel of concern in my belly. "*Pronto.*"

"I'm letting you know that we had an unwelcome visitor today," he says.

That concern ratchets up. "Is everyone at the house all right?"

"*Si, Don Conte.*"

"Well, who the fuck was it?"

"She said her name was Electra. It was on her ID, and well... we know she is a friend of yours."

What the hell? "And you let her in?"

There is hesitation on the other end of the phone, and I don't envy him his concern about my wrath because I'm pissed. "We had no reason to believe that she was unwelcome here."

I grind my teeth. I have Aria, a woman I want to make my wife, and they think Electra is welcome at my home? Even if I were a man to cheat, I wouldn't do it in front of Aria.

"When has Electra ever been to my house?" My anger is palpable through the phone.

"We are aware that you're friends and... uh... she had important information for you."

"But I'm not there." I rub my temple. Surely, my head of security is smarter than this.

"Yes, I know. Had I been the one at the gate at the moment, I would have sent her away. But—"

"Never mind. Is she gone?"

"Yes, sir. We were careful but insistent that she leave."

Careful? What the fuck does that mean? My phone is buzzing, indicating I have another call. I glance quickly at it and realize it's Roberta. "Make sure she doesn't come back."

I end the call and pick up Roberta's. She's talking a mile a minute.

"Slow down. What happened?" The concern in her voice has me grabbing my jacket and preparing to leave.

"Electra was going through Aria's things."

"What do you mean?" I give a nod to Bruno, who acknowledges it and takes over the meeting while I leave.

"She was in the closet. We didn't let her in, Don Conte. I don't know how she got in."

I understand that part of Roberta's rapid speech is from fear of my wrath. "Is Aria okay?"

"She is shaken. Signora Fontana is here."

Okay, good. All I can see in my mind's eye is Aria packing a bag and heading back to New York. "Try not to let Aria leave." I'm in my car, glad that I drove and hoping Aria isn't preparing to leave. I can only imagine what she's thinking. What the hell did Electra say to her? I want to hunt Electra down and find out what she's up to.

I'm speeding back to the villa and decide to use the few minutes to find out what Electra is playing at.

"You finally call, Daddy."

"What the fuck are you up to, Electra?"

"Didn't your new pet tell you? You're going to be a daddy. If you want to keep her, I have no problem with that, but I'm going to be the woman of the house. You need to get her out."

My hands flex and then wrap around the steering wheel as my brain scrambles to figure out what she's talking about. "Have you been drinking?"

She lets out an exasperated breath. "I haven't been drinking because I'm pregnant. With your child, Luca. Try to get rid of me now."

These are very dangerous words. I know plenty of powerful men who would absolutely get rid of an inconvenient woman, especially one making demands. Electra is fortunate that I'm not one of them. I'm not sure that she knows that, though.

"You're playing a dangerous game, Electra."

"It's not a game. I'm carrying your child."

"That's impossible." I'm doing mental math to figure out if it is possible. I haven't been with Electra in a long time. Not since I made the decision to return to New York and help Niko and Lucia with the war they had going on against Lucia's father. I think back to when I saw Electra at the club recently. The clothing around her belly was loose. Had she been hiding a pregnancy?

It doesn't matter, I tell myself. I've always used a condom when I was with Electra. I've used a condom with every woman I've ever been with, except Aria. It's reckless, I know. Probably misogynistic too. But I can't imagine being with Aria with barriers. She's mine and I'm hers, and any child born of our coming together will be blessed and welcome into the Conte family.

"Your people very rudely shoved me out, but I will be back, Luca. You need to tell them."

"You need to watch your tone with me, Electra. The game you're playing is very dangerous. If you continue to threaten my home, to threaten Aria, you're going to have a problem."

"You wouldn't dare kill your unborn child."

"No, but someday, that child's going to be born, and then we'll test and find out that it's not mine."

She is silent, and I think she's finally understanding that she is not going to bully her way into my home, into my life.

"This child is yours. You have to marry me and get rid of that American. I'll do it for you if I have to."

"If the baby is mine, I will do right by the child, but you will never be the mistress of my home. You will never be my wife. If you ever come near Aria again, your child will be an orphan." I click the off button and roll my shoulders, uncomfortable with the threat I just delivered. I don't kill women, but I won't tolerate any threats against Aria.

I speed through the gate and skid to a stop in front of the house. I rush in, calling out for Aria. Roberta appears immediately and tells me that Aria is outside on the terrace. I make a beeline to her, and when I reach her, I want to pull her up and take her in my arms to make sure she's all right.

Her expression stops me. Her eyes are narrow in accusation. It hurts and frustrates me that she still doesn't trust me. But I remind myself that an ex lover of mine broke into my house. I'd probably have doubts too if things were reversed.

I grab a chair from the table and put it in front of her, sitting down and leaning forward toward her. "Are you all right?"

"How did she get in the house?"

"She—"

Aria holds up a hand to stop me. "She got in because your men know to let her in. Because she's been here. What is going on, Luca? Is this one of those situations in which you marry one woman for her pedigree but you get your rocks off with a mistress?"

"No." I'm feeling desperate and it's uncomfortable. I'm resenting Aria for making me feel this way. I've done nothing wrong. "Electra has never been in my home. Never in my bed. I don't know why she was allowed in except for the fact that it's known that she was once a lover of mine. But that is all she was."

Aria purses her lips and tilts her head to the side. "Perhaps they let her in because she's carrying your child."

My head is shaking before she finishes the words. "It's not my child. You can think whatever fucked up thing you want to think about me, Aria. But know this. That baby, if there really is one, is not mine."

Her expression softens momentarily, but then she pulls it back in as if she doesn't want to believe me. "How can you be so sure?"

"For one, I always use a condom."

"You don't with me."

"That's because you and I belong to each other. Think about it, Aria. I am not a reckless man. Except maybe when it comes to you. For you, I've taken on the most powerful Don in America. For you, I'm prepared to give everything I am, my very soul."

I can see the tug-of-war in her eyes, of wanting to believe me but afraid to do so.

"I'm going to get to the bottom of this, Aria. I will deal with Electra—"

"How?" Concern laces her eyes. I remember that she saw me kill a man she believed to be an innocent homeless man.

"That's not code for I'm going to kill her. But she will be dealt with."

"She got into the house, and nobody saw her. She could get in and slit my throat."

The vision of that is more than I can bear. I reach out, taking Aria's hands in mine. "I won't let that happen."

"How can you stop it? She was in my closet."

She's right. Perhaps I've underestimated Electra. Between her and dealing with Sabini's rogue men, now may not be the safest time for Aria to be here with me.

"You should go to New York. Go to Lucia's baby shower."

Her eyes round, clearly not expecting me to say that. "You want me to leave?" She starts to tug her hands away, but I grip them tighter.

"Hell no. I want you here with me, by my side for always. But I want you to feel safe. And I know that your family is important to you."

"Come with me." She leans forward, her hands gripping mine, and I feel it like a lifeline.

"You know I can't."

"Niko won't kill you. He might want to beat you up..."

My lips twitch upward. "It's not just Niko. I need to handle Electra and some other business from the fallout of Sabini's demise. You understand, don't you?"

She nods. "Okay."

Nothing has changed. She's still holding my hands. But all of a sudden, I feel like she's moving away from me. Who knows what will happen when she's in New York? Perhaps all the glitter that shines in her eyes toward me will clear and she'll realize that I'm not the romantic hero she's been wanting. Or maybe Niko will force her to stay in New York.

But her safety is more important. "I'll make the arrangements for a flight to New York."

She shakes her head. "Newark. I'll go stay with Lucy and Donovan."

I nod. I like the idea slightly better than her staying with Niko.

She smiles, her hands cradling my face. She can see my unease, and it's like a balm on my heart.

"I'll come back."

I kiss her and pray that it's true.

LATER, when Aria is in bed, I meet with Bruno to figure out what to do about Electra.

"I can't believe she got into the house. Aria is afraid she'll slit her throat in her sleep." I run my fingers through my hair in frustration. I let my dick get me into this trouble by fucking her in the first place. Now she could ruin my tentative hold on Aria.

"I'll make sure security knows to keep her out."

"Is she really pregnant? Who has she been fucking?"

Bruno looks down, shifts uncomfortably.

"Oh, hell... you?"

He winces. "You were in New York... the second time."

"Could this baby be yours?"

He shrugs.

I feel a twinge of frustration at Bruno's lack of caution. Not at fucking a woman I used to fuck, but at not being more careful to avoid a pregnancy.

"In retrospect, it was probably a set up. She came on pretty strong, and well..."

I hold my hand up. "I don't need details." I know all about Electra's powers of seduction. "What I need is to keep her away from Aria."

Bruno nods solemnly, then suggests, "Maybe I should marry her."

The idea amuses me, but I can see the sincerity in his expression. The truth is, I don't want to lose my right-hand man, but getting Electra away from Aria means I may have to let him go. I have some business in the south that I could hand over to him.

"How would you feel about taking over the Gioia Tauro?" I say of our import-export business in southern Italy.

"I can see her becoming the village queen."

He seems genuinely interested in this idea. "Do you love her?"

He shakes his head. "No, but I'll do right by her and the child." His lips twitch upward. "I kind of like the idea of being a dad."

Memories of Aria holding a toddler flash through my mind, and I find myself wondering about fatherhood as well. The thought both thrills and terrifies me. I just don't want to be Electra's baby daddy.

I smile, seeing a new side to him. "Marrying Electra could work, although I hate to let you go."

"I'm sorry."

I wave his apology away. "I'm not upset that you slept with her. You should learn to use a condom, though."

His cheeks flush. "It was a little—"

Again, I hold my hand up. "I don't want the details. Take care of it. I need to arrange for Aria to go to New York for a week or so. I want this all cleared up by the time she returns."

Bruno arches a brow. "Is that wise? Don Leone will likely keep her from coming back."

Agitation slides through me knowing he's right. "She plans to stay with Lucia."

He doesn't look convinced about that answer.

"I need Aria to feel safe, and she needs to see her family." And maybe by letting her go, Niko will see that I have no intention of keeping her from him. Maybe he'll then bless our relationship.

"I'll deal with Electra tonight."

I nod. "See that you convince her to make this move, Bruno. I mean it. I can't have her fucking things up with Aria."

His brow furrows. "What if I can't?"

I suck in a breath knowing he's asking how far to go with Electra. "She's stubborn, but smart. She wants a lavish life. We can make that happen. She'll take that deal over managing in the club."

When he leaves, I make arrangements for a flight to Newark for Aria. That feeling like I'm sending her away and won't see her again fills me with dread. My instinct is to force her to stay. To lock her in a gilded cage to keep her safe and with me.

What is that saying? If you love something, set it free? So I'm going to let her go and hope like hell that she comes back to me.

22

ARIA

The next morning, after thinking about what it will be like to return home, I decide I don't want to stay with Lucy and Donovan either. While they may not try to keep me in the United States, they are an extension of my brother and I don't want to be under anyone's watchful eyes.

When I tell Luca my decision over breakfast, he frowns. "You should stay with your Family. It's safer there."

I shake my head. "I don't want to be cooped up in Niko's penthouse or with Lucy and Donovan. I don't need a babysitter. I want to be on my own."

Luca sighs, running a hand through his dark hair. "It's not about babysitting, it's about being safe. You need protection."

"You can provide me protection."

He puts his hand over mine. "I can't come with you. You know that."

"So send someone with me. Didn't you say I'm yours now?" I wonder if I'm asking too much.

Luca looks conflicted. I know it's hard for him to suggest I stay with Niko, the man who has opposed our relationship from the start. But I also see the logic in his concern.

Finally, he nods. "Okay. I'll send Bruno with you."

I'm a little surprised that Luca is sending his most trusted associate to watch over me, especially with so much going on right now. "Don't you need him? You can send someone else."

Luca presses his hand on my cheek. "Aria, you are my number one treasure. I won't take any chances when it comes to your wellbeing." His eyes burn with a fierce intensity that makes my heart skip a beat. "Bruno is the best man for the job, and I need him to keep you safe while you're away from me."

"Thank you." I lean in and kiss him, feeling happy and cared for. There haven't been any exchanges of words of love, but there's no denying that I feel my place is here with Luca.

THE NEXT DAY, I fly to New York with Bruno. It wasn't that long ago when he was escorting me from New York to Italy, yet in many ways, it feels like a lifetime ago. So much has happened, some of it not so good. But I'm stronger now, more sure of myself and what I want, not from a dreamer's perspective like before. I'm more grounded in reality.

As we drive through the city streets, I can't help but feel a sense of independence, even with Bruno by my side as my protection. This isn't the sheltered life I once knew under Niko's thumb. I'm making my own choices now, even if I'm still not entirely free.

I check into the hotel on Fifth Avenue not far from Central Park. I have a lovely two-bedroom suite, although Bruno states that he'll sleep on the couch so he can better watch the door for intruders.

The following day, I prepare for Lucy's baby shower. It may be odd, but I want to look as different as I feel inside. Confident. Mature. I don't want them to see a petulant, spoiled young woman, as I'm sure Niko sees me.

I select a pastel yellow dress and style my dark hair into a loose chignon bun. As I apply my makeup in the hotel mirror, I can't help but feel a flutter of nerves. It's been so long since I've seen my family and friends.

Dressed and ready, I leave the hotel with Bruno. He walks beside me, his eyes scanning the area with a worried expression. I know he's concerned about Niko's reaction to my return. He's outnumbered in my brother's territory.

"I don't think Niko will do anything to you," I say as we approach the car Lucy sent for us.

"It's not me I'm worried about." He gives me a kind smile. "If I don't return to Italy with you, Luca's heart will break."

His words send a flutter through my heart. It also boosts my confidence. I'm not a runaway brat. I'm a woman who chooses to be with the man she loves and who cares deeply for her too.

I slide into the back of the sleek, black car with Bruno sitting next to me. I take a deep breath, trying to push away the anxiety. This is my family, and I'm here to celebrate Lucy's coming motherhood. No matter what happens, I won't let Niko or the Mafia drama ruin this day for me.

When we arrive at the lavish downtown venue, I step out of the car. The building is decked out in elegant floral arrangements and glimmering lights, a clear sign that Donovan has spared no expense for Lucy's baby shower.

As I make my way inside with Bruno close at hand, I spot familiar faces. Kate is absolutely glowing, cradling her newborn daughter,

Sophie, while Elena juggles her twins, Niccolo and Angelica. I rush over to them, enveloping them in warm hugs.

"Aria! We've missed you so much," Kate exclaims, her eyes shining with joy.

"I've missed you too." I peer down at the sleeping baby, my heart swelling with affection. "She's beautiful, Kate." I look over at Liam, my brother's friend since childhood.

"Hey, Liam." I give him a hug.

"Aria. It's good to see you."

Kate and Liam's relationship is proof to me that true love can prevail even in the most difficult of situations. Yes, Lucy and Donovan, and Niko and Elena, have endured challenges, but to me, Kate's not being from our world and Liam's closed off emotions should have gotten in the way. Love, true love, does make a difference, even if life is messy and complicated.

Elena chimes in, bouncing one of the twins on her hip. "You look good, Aria. Happy."

"I am." I glance around, wanting Niko to have heard her statement. But I don't see him.

"You'll have to catch us up on everything."

"There's so much." I figure I'll avoid mentioning Sabini, which they no doubt know about from Niko. I'll keep the latest about Electra to myself as well. "Where's Lucy?"

"You can't miss me." Lucy's voice is laced with irritation. "I'm like a beached whale."

"A beautiful beached whale." Donovan stands beside her, a fond smile on his face as he rubs her back.

I give them both a hug, then I look beyond them, expecting Niko.

Donovan, who's been like an uncle to me, presses his hand on my cheek. "He's not here. He doesn't want to ruin the day."

I scowl. "Are you saying he can't help himself and he'll be a jerk if he sees me?"

Donovan's eyes are sad. "He's doing the best he can."

Not good enough, I think, but I put that aside. I'm going to enjoy my friends no matter what Niko does or doesn't do.

"Shall we let the fun and games begin?" Elena says. Her nanny comes over to help with the twins as Elena takes charge of the shower activities.

"Does it involve waddling? That's about all I'm good for," Lucy complains.

"Goodness, Lucy, where did your sense of fun go? You're such a whiner," Elena jokes.

Donovan chuckles, wrapping an arm around Lucy's shoulders. "My warrior princess scares even the fiercest made men in the city."

"Yeah, well, you carry around a bowling ball in your belly and tell me that won't make you grumpy," Lucy says.

"I did. I carried two." Elena arches a brow.

"Everyone knows you're the nicer sister," Lucy responds.

I smile, happy to be home... no, not home. My home is now in Italy. But it's good to be back with my friends. They're the same. Happy. Funny. Loving people.

Elena leads the way with activities until it's time to eat. After lunch, we continue to chat. I hold Kate's baby girl, gently rocking her, feeling a surge of emotion. I want one. Maybe not right away, but someday. Does Luca want kids?

"She's so precious," I murmur, my gaze fixed on the sleeping baby.

Elena sidles up and sits next to me. "You look so natural holding her, Aria."

I glance up at her, my heart swelling with affection for my sister-in-law. I'm so happy Niko found her and had the good sense to marry her. If only he'd develop good sense around me.

"I've missed this, being around family."

Elena's expression shifts to one of empathy. "You can come home, if you want."

I shift, as does my mood. "I'm happy with Luca."

She nods. "I just want to be sure that your motivation is to be with Luca."

I frown. "What else would it be?"

"To escape Niko."

Not long ago, I'd completely dismissed her comment, but after everything I've been through, I take a moment to consider it.

Finally, I answer, "I've never seen Luca as my escape. I'm with him because I want to be. And he wants to be with me. Do you know he asked Niko for permission... which is crazy in this day and age, but—"

She laughs. "Our men retain some antiquated ways, although I think it's rooted in respect."

"So you do know?"

She sighs. "Yes. And I don't necessarily agree with Niko, but he's—"

"I know. He's the boss of everyone." I shake my head.

"He's doing what he thinks is right." Elena's tone turns defensive.

"For whom?" I arch a brow, not wanting to get into a confrontation but also not liking being told that Niko has to make decisions for me. I'm not inept.

"Aria—"

"I know you all see me as an immature Mafia princess. Yes, I was sheltered. Yes, there's much about the world I don't know. Do you want to know what I do know? I know my brother sent me away when I was ten years old after losing my other brother and mother. I know that he kept me away after school and college. I know he never told me about you and the babies. How is that right for anyone but him?"

Her expression turns to sympathy. "I can see that you've felt abandoned. Niko has made many mistakes in his life, but you can't think he doesn't love you and doesn't want what's best for you."

I shrug. "How do I know that?"

She watches me for a moment. "Is Luca good to you?"

I nod. "Very. He's sweet and kind. Niko says no to me all the time. No way he'd let me go to Luca. But Luca supported my coming here, even knowing Niko could find a way to prevent me from returning to Italy. Luca cares about what I think and feel. Niko doesn't care about anything but bossing me around."

"That's not completely true. Niko is overprotective, but he does love you and wants you to be happy."

"Then tell him Luca makes me happy. I love Luca with all my heart."

"Does he feel the same?"

Luca's never said the words, but he's said other things to make me think he cares for me. "We were supposed to get married."

Her eyes widen.

"Things happened, so it's been…" I don't know if it's been canceled or postponed. "It hasn't happened yet."

"And you didn't invite family?"

"Why would I invite Niko? He's not even here, and it's because of me."

She looks away for a moment. I know I've hit the nail on the head.

"I don't want to ruin Lucy's shower. Just know that I'm happy with Luca. Is that enough?"

She nods. "That's more than enough. If Luca truly makes you happy, then I'll support you, no matter what."

I feel a weight lift from my shoulders, and I lean in to hug Elena tightly. "Thank you, Elena. It means the world to me to have your support." Not that she'll change Niko's mind because I doubt she can, but I have at least one ally.

AFTER THE PARTY, I make my way back to the hotel with Bruno's watchful eyes keeping me safe. I check my phone and see a missed call from Luca. I press the redial, eager to hear his voice. I hear it, but it's his voicemail message. I do the math to figure out the time in Italy. It's nearly midnight. Perhaps he's sleeping. I can't stop the image of Electra in my room coming to mind and making the leap to her being in bed with him. I shake it from my mind. I trust him. I trust him. Am I talking myself into that?

We reach the hotel suite.

"Thank you for escorting me, Bruno. I'm sure it's not as exciting as your normal duties." I use the keycard to unlock the door.

"I don't know. Lucia is scarier than I remember."

I laugh, and he laughs with me. "I forgot you know her," I say.

"She was very good to Luca's father. Everyone respects and admires her for that."

Stepping into the hotel suite, I go to my room to change. Once in yoga pants and a T-shirt, I sit on the bed and try to call Luca again. Again, the call goes to voicemail. Worry grows. I pace the room, my mind racing with possibilities. What if something has happened to him? What if one of Sabini's men made a move against Luca? The thought of Luca being in danger sends a shiver down my spine.

Sinking down onto the edge of the bed, I try to calm my racing thoughts. I need to be level-headed, to think this through rationally. Perhaps Luca is simply busy, caught up in some important business matters. Maybe he's just asleep. There's no need to jump to the worst-case scenario.

Still, I can't shake the uneasy feeling that something is wrong. I exit the bedroom and find Bruno on the couch looking at his phone.

"Have you heard from Luca?" I ask.

He glances up. "Sure."

"Now?"

He studies me. "Is there a problem?"

"He's not answering his phone."

"He could be at the club. It's hard to hear there. Or maybe asleep." Bruno doesn't sound concerned, so I shouldn't be.

I nod. "Okay. If you want dinner, you can order room service."

"Are you hungry?"

I shake my head. "I ate a lot at the shower. I think I'll take a soak in the tub and call it a night. I've got a shopping day planned tomorrow."

He nods, and I suspect he'd rather be facing the enemy than chaperoning me around boutique shops.

"Will you let me know if you hear from him?" I ask.

"Of course. But don't worry."

That's easier said than done. As I sit in the bubbly hot water of the tub, I realize that worry is a part of this world. I imagine Elena and Kate worry all the time when Niko and Liam are working. Maybe Lucy worries too, although she's such a badass, I'm sure she's right alongside Donovan when shit goes down.

For a moment, I wonder if that's the type of stress I want in my life. I think about what I could do if I wasn't with a man in organized crime. But the idea of not being with Luca feels much worse. I'd rather worry about him than try to live a life without him.

I realize that I haven't told him how I feel. I've had sex with him, and I've acted like an impulsive, jealous ninny. What can he possibly make of that? I need to use words to let him know I love him. I need to do better to show him that I'm committed to staying. He is my future. As much as I want my friends and even Niko in my life, it's time I stake my claim to my life. To my love. To Luca.

23

LUCA

The house feels empty with Aria gone. I fill my time with work that needs to be done, but I'm using it as a distraction more than my job.

Roberta and the other staff seem to feel it as well. I can hear them talking about how they miss Aria's attempts to speak Italian.

At night, with nothing to occupy my mind, is the worst. The silence echoes through the house, accentuating her absence.

Tonight, I'm at my desk, feeling lonely. I call Aria, needing to hear her voice, but then I remember the time in New York and realize she's at her baby shower. I scrape my hands over my face and prepare for another long night of missing her.

My phone rings, and I grab it, hoping she's calling me back.

"Don Conte?" a guard at the gate greets.

"Yes."

"The woman... the one we're not to let in is at the gate."

So send her away, I think. "What does she want?"

"It has to do with the child." His voice is tentative. He knows he risks my anger by interrupting me with this when my order was to keep her away. I suspect it's that she's pregnant that has them calling.

"Keep her there. I'll come out." I make my way outside, bracing myself for the confrontation.

Electra stands there, her eyes pleading. "Luca, please, you have to listen to me. The baby is yours, I know it is."

I cross my arms, my jaw tightening. "We've been through this. I've told you, I won't be a part of your games."

"But it's the truth!" she insists, her voice rising. "The child is yours, I swear it."

I raise a hand, silencing her. "What about Bruno?"

Electra waves a dismissive hand. "It doesn't matter. Bruno means nothing to me. You're the one I want, Luca. We belong together."

"You'd really take his child from him?" I'm not surprised. "Why would I want a woman who'd do such a thing?"

She scoffs. "You're no saint."

I shake my head. "No. I don't care about earning wings. You should keep that in mind when dealing with me." It's a veiled threat. One that I wouldn't be able to carry out, but she doesn't know that.

She steps back, telling me she understands.

"Bruno is making you a good offer. I suggest you take it. We both know the truth. You don't want me. You want my money and the life-style I can provide. That's all this has ever been about."

She moves toward me again, her hand reaching out to touch me. "That's not true, Luca. I love you. I've always loved you. This child is ours, I swear it."

I shake my head, unwilling to be drawn in by her manipulations. "Spare me the lies. This has nothing to do with me." I think of Aria. How she looks at me like I'm a superhero. Except for that time she saw me kill Sabini's man. It gutted me that I'd fallen in her estimation. But since then, I feel that she sees me as who I am, wants me as who I am, not my power or influence or money.

Electra's expression hardens, her desperation giving way to anger. "How dare you! I've given you everything, Luca. My body, my loyalty, my heart. And you repay me by throwing me aside for some American whore?"

My jaw tightens, and it takes all my effort not to strike out. "Watch yourself, Electra. You're precariously close to stepping over the line. You will not talk about her to me... or to anyone. Do you understand?"

She must see the lethalness inside me as she again steps back.

"If you're smart, you'll take Bruno's offer. It gets you what you want."

She crosses her arms. "Bruno is a sap."

I narrow my eyes at her as I realize the truth. "Is he even the father?"

She looks away and shrugs.

"Is he!" I demand.

"I don't know. Maybe."

"Maybe? Who else could it be?"

"You—"

"Not me. Don't bullshit me. Who else?"

"Rocco."

"Rocco, as in Rocco Perotta?" Rocco works for me near Gioia Tauro. He makes regular trips to Rome for business. In my mind, this is a good thing. Perhaps I can keep Bruno here and still send her away.

"Yes." She gives me a look of disdain. "He's got a bigger dick than you."

I ignore the jab at my manhood. She's lucky I can. I know plenty of men who'd strike her for that.

"Good, then you should be happy with him."

She realizes her mistake. "Luca, please—"

"I'm done with this conversation. Here's what can happen. I'll talk to Rocco. You'll move south. Marry him or not, I don't care. But either way, I'll make sure you have a nice home and a lavish lifestyle. Your other option is that you continue the way you do now, working while trying to raise a child on your own."

She stares at me, her eyes narrowed. "So that's it, then? I either accept your terms and disappear, or I get nothing? What kind of choice is that?"

"The only one I'm willing to give you," I reply, my voice unwavering. "You can have a lavish life with all the comforts and luxuries you crave. Or you can have nothing. The choice is yours."

Her shoulders slump in defeat. But just as quickly, it's replaced by a steely determination. "I won't give up on you, Luca. You and I, we're meant to be together. I'll fight for you, no matter what."

I sigh, knowing this conversation is going nowhere. "Then you've made your choice. I expect you to continue your work at the club. Note that if you come back here ever again, if you go near Aria, there will be consequences."

She lets out a frustrated growl. "Fine. I'll go with Rocco."

I nod, unsurprised by her decision. "Very well. I'll have my men handle the situation. You'll be taken care of as long as you leave and never come back."

With that, I turn and head back inside, the weight of the evening's events dragging me down. But it's Aria's absence that is the worst. It's a constant ache, and I long for her return.

The next day, I'm restless at breakfast. Roberta must notice as she asks whether Aria is coming back soon.

"Of course," I state with a certainty that I don't feel. I start to question if sending Aria away was necessary, considering how I've gotten rid of Electra. Perhaps Electra wasn't such a threat, after all.

It's worse that I haven't heard from Aria. Our calls keep missing each other. Or maybe she's ignoring them. Perhaps she's decided she wants to stay in New York. Hell, maybe Niko has taken her phone and forced her to stay. Texts from Bruno don't indicate that, but they've been too brief to know for sure what's going on.

I pace my office, running a hand through my hair in frustration. I know Aria is safe with Bruno by her side, but the distance between us feels like an uncrossable chasm. It's unbearable.

I grab my phone and call Paolo. "I've got to leave the country. You're in charge until I or Bruno return." It's an impulsive decision. But at this point, I care less about how my business might implode than I do about seeing Aria.

"Is everything alright?" Paolo asks, his voice laced with concern.

"I need to check on Aria. Can you handle this responsibility?"

"Of course." His voice hints at nervousness at the weight of what I've just bestowed on him. I hope he can manage it.

When I end the call, I rush upstairs and pack a bag. I arrange for a plane during the drive to the airport. Before takeoff, I attempt to call Aria again, but she doesn't answer. I can't bring myself to leave a message, the fear that she's ghosting me too heavy to put into words. I don't call Bruno for the same reason. I'm too worried that he'll confirm my worst fear. That she's staying in New York.

As the plane ascends, I gaze out the window, my mind consumed by thoughts of Aria. I feel a tightness in my chest, a longing that I haven't experienced since the first time I had to leave her. Aria has become more than just a prize to be won. She's seeped into my heart, my soul.

I reflect on our time together, the way her laughter lights up a room. The way she interacts with my staff, who delight in her and her efforts to speak to them. The way her touch sets my soul on fire. I've never felt this way about anyone before, and the thought of her choosing to stay in New York, away from me, fills me with a sense of dread.

I've always prided myself on my ability to get what I want, but with Aria, it's different. She's not just some pawn in my game of power and influence. She's a woman I've come to care for deeply, a woman I want by my side, not just as my wife, but as my partner.

I think about the lessons my father taught me. He told me to find a wife to be my other half. To be the source of my power. Aria is that woman. Unfortunately, my father failed to tell me how to make this woman mine. Regret seeps in as I realize I may not have done enough to show her the depth of my feelings. I've been so focused on claiming her. Not that I haven't been kind or conceding in many cases, but I haven't told her how I feel. How she is my source of power.

As the plane soars higher, I make a silent vow that when I see Aria again, I'll pour my heart out to her. I'll show her the side of me that I've kept hidden, the side that yearns for her affection, her trust, her love. I'll do whatever it takes to prove my commitment to her, to convince her that her place is by my side, not back in New York.

The minutes on the flight tick by, each one feeling like an eternity. I can't sit still, my leg bouncing with nervous energy. I need to see her, to hold her, to reassure myself that she hasn't slipped through my fingers. The thought of losing her, of her choosing a life without me, is too much to bear.

24

ARIA

Retail therapy is real. But as much as I love having new things, the therapeutic aspect is being with my friends. For the most part, we peruse baby shops, buying things for Lucy's baby. But I also buy items for my niece and nephew and for Kate's baby. We have lunch at a nice rooftop restaurant where I soak up the sun and the sounds of the city. I miss this place, but not so much that I feel a pull to it. The pull is to Luca. I miss his villa by the sea. I miss Roberta and the other staff who I'm sure are amused by my inability to speak to them but are patient with me. I even miss Bianca. She'd have loved today's shopping spree. Maybe someday, I can bring her to New York to join us. Mostly, I miss Luca. I miss the way he looks at me like I'm the center of the world. I miss hearing his voice and am trying hard not to let my mind think the worst about our inability to connect.

When the afternoon is done, Bruno escorts me back to the hotel.

"You look like you enjoyed yourself," he says next to me in the car.

I glance at him, wondering if he's feeling out whether or not I plan to stay instead of returning to Italy. "I did. It distracted me from not talking to Luca. Is he okay?"

Bruno nods but then looks out the window. It sends a sliver of concern through me.

"What's going on?"

"Nothing."

"Does it have to do with Electra? Is she still trying to get her claws in him?" My tone and expression are tough, but inside, I realize I have some fear that Bianca and the wives are right. Their men like to have extra women on the side.

"Electra is dealt with."

"How?"

Bruno shifts uncomfortably. That concern inside me grows.

"What, Bruno? What has Luca done to deal with Electra?" I'm terrified of both possibilities—that he killed her or he's taken her to his bed.

"I will take her south."

I gape. "Is that code for send her to hell?"

His eyes widen in surprise. "No. It means I'll marry her and move her south to run things for Don Conte there."

"You'll marry her?" This makes no sense.

He looks out the window again. "The baby is probably mine."

"Probably?" Did Luca and Bruno share her?

"It's not Luca's, if that is concerning you."

I believe him, and because I do, relief fills me. "Do you love her?"

"No. But I like the idea of being a father."

I smile. "I think you'll be a good one. You've been taking good care of me."

His smile to me is genuine. "*Grazia*."

We arrive at the hotel and head up to my suite. I plan to try again to call Luca. I may have to cut this trip short if I don't talk to him soon.

Bruno opens the door, and I step in. Movement near the window has me sucking in a breath of air.

Bruno must have seen it too as he steps in front of me and pulls his gun. "Who's there?"

Luca steps from the shadows, his arms up in surrender.

"Luca?" I ask, both confused and joyful.

A warm smile spreads across his face as he moves his arms open for an embrace. "Aria."

I feel a deep sense of belonging and throw my arms around him, kissing him passionately. Luca returns the kiss, his strong arms enveloping me.

"What are you doing here?"

"I couldn't be away from you one minute more."

I turn to Bruno. "Did you know he was coming?"

"I did not."

That surprises me. I look at Luca.

He gives me a sheepish smile. "I acted impulsively. I missed you, and so I got on a plane and here I am."

"I thought you couldn't come."

"I decided I'd risk it to see you. Paolo is watching things, although I'd like for you to return to Italy, Bruno."

"I should stay and protect you," Bruno says.

"I'd feel better with you managing things in Italy. Oh, and that issue we discussed before? It's resolved. Rocco Perotta is dealing with it."

Bruno's brows knit together.

"It's Rocco's *responsibility*," Luca says.

Bruno sighs, almost looking disappointed. "*Grazia*. I'll take my leave."

When Bruno leaves, I turn my attention to Luca. "What's that about?"

"Just an issue that's dealt with."

"Is this about Electra? He told me he was going to marry her because he was her baby's father."

Luca arches a brow, but his smile is amused. "He told you that, did he?"

"Yes. I think he likes me."

Luca laughs. "Everyone likes you, *Mio Angelo*. As far as Bruno, it turns out he isn't the father."

"Rocco is?"

Luca nods.

"Who is Rocco?"

"He works for me at a port in southern Italy. Is this what we're going to talk about? I've flown all the way from Italy, risking life and limb."

I loop my arms around his neck. "What would you rather talk about?"

"How much I missed you?" He pulls me close, his lips brushing against my forehead.

"I missed you too." I kiss him, coaxing him into one of those molten hot lip locks that make my toes curl. His hands slide down my back, covering my backside and pulling me close. His erection is hard against my belly. It sends liquid heat to my pussy.

"Perhaps we can talk later," he murmurs against my neck.

"Yes." My fingers undo the buttons of his shirt. Like a switch is flipped, our hands are a flurry of movement. Our clothes lie in our wake as we move to my room.

"I'm glad you're here," I say as I tug him on the bed over me.

"It fills my heart to hear you say that." He kisses me again, firmly, fully, passionately.

My body is on fire with need. "Luca, now. Please, now..."

"Normally, I'd like to take my time, but I find I'm as desperate as you, *Mio Angelo*." He levers back, sitting on his heels. He tugs my legs over his thighs, positioning his dick at my entrance.

His eyes are filled with a wild heat, but also with something more. Something I hope is love. Our gazes hold as he thrusts inside. Pleasure erupts. I arch back, my eyes closing to manage the delicious sensations.

"Watch me, Aria. Watch me make you come."

It takes a great deal of effort, but I open my eyes, meeting Luca's. They're intense, filled with heat and passion. His fingers grip my hips as he moves in and out, steadily building tension inside me.

"Do you feel me, *Mio Angelo*?"

"Yes."

"I'm in you. A part of you."

"Yes."

He lets out a feral growl. "Only me. You're mine." His thrusts become harder, faster, and I can barely breathe as I'm pushed to the edge.

"Only me. You're mine," I repeat back to him, not wanting to be simply his belonging. I want us to belong to each other.

He gives me a slight nod. "Come, Aria. Take me to heaven with you."

He drives in, grinding against me, hitting the spot that sends me rocketing out to oblivion. I cry out, my body going taut.

"Fuck... yes." He lets go, his body rocking, bucking, filling me with a part of him. Together we move, our bodies coming together like they're made for each other.

He collapses over me, his breath hard and heavy against my neck. "I love you, *Mio Angelo*."

My heart stops. I turn my head toward him. He lifts his, looking at me. For the first time ever, I see vulnerability. I realize he's given me something he's never given anyone.

"I love you, Luca."

Relief spreads on his face and he kisses me. This is all I've ever wanted. I understand that there is still much for us to work through. Life isn't always smooth sailing. But with his words, I feel like I've found my place. I fall asleep in his arms feeling like I'm finally home.

I WAKE up still wrapped in Luca's strong embrace. A contented sigh escapes my lips.

Luca stirs beside me, pressing a gentle kiss to my forehead. "Good morning, my love," he murmurs, his voice rough with sleep.

I smile up at him, my fingers tracing the defined lines of his jaw. "Good morning." I nestle closer, reveling in the warmth of his body.

My stomach growls.

Luca chuckles. "Hungry?"

I smile sheepishly. "Apparently."

Luca reaches for the phone, ordering a decadent breakfast from room service. The simple gesture makes my heart swell with affection. He always takes such good care of me. Not that I need to be taken care of, but it's nice to feel nurtured. I should probably do the same for him.

We kiss for long moments, but then Luca rises from bed, getting a robe from the closet. "If I don't stop now, our breakfast will arrive and get cold."

It would be worth it to me, but I get out of bed too, slipping on a second robe Luca holds up for me.

We move to the main area of the suite just as a knock comes on the door.

"They are fast," Luca says as he goes to open it. He pulls the door open and immediately is shoved back. I gasp as I see a man with murderous eyes bearing down on Luca.

25

LUCA

I'm not usually taken off guard, but in this case, I am. I stumble back and am ready to kill the intruder.

"Niko!" Aria yells as she comes to my side.

Niko's eyes take in me and Aria, both in robes. There's no doubt that he knows what I've been doing with Aria. He might have pretended before that she was untouched since I put her in a guestroom when he visited. Now there is no such pretense, and I can see that he's unhappy. Well, too fucking bad.

I pull myself together, remembering my father's words of wisdom about control and respect being the key to power. I have to consider that he knew I'd be here, in which case his men are following me or Aria and reporting back. Men who are likely close by.

"Niko," I say, keeping my tone even. "This is a surprise."

"We need to talk."

"Alright." I make a gesture to let him in.

"No. My office." He glances at my robe again. "Thirty minutes."

"No." Aria steps into his space. "I don't know why you're here, but you have no right to butt into my life. What Luca and I do is none of your business."

"You're my responsibility," he snaps at her.

I put my arm around her. "Not anymore. She's mine."

In a surprise move, Aria knocks my arm off her shoulder and steps away, looking at both me and Niko as if she'd like to slap us.

"I'm not your property. I make my own decisions."

Niko's jaw tightens. "That's not the world you live in, Aria. You know this."

Her hands fist at her sides. I think she might actually take a swing at us. "You gave Elena a choice." She turns to me. "You gave Lucia a choice. You even gave me a choice. I made it, Luca, but that doesn't mean I'm your property."

"It doesn't have anything to do with property, Aria." Niko's tone is patronizing. Like he's talking to a child. "As my sister, your life could be in danger. Same with Luca. Fucking hell, you know that. You've seen it. You experienced it. I know you think you're in love, but I don't approve, and like or not, I'm the head of the Family."

What he's saying is true. I hate that I'm in agreement with him.

She looks at both of us as if she doesn't recognize us. She turns back to Niko. "I really don't like you."

Niko's eyes flash with something I can't quite define. Regret? But it quickly leaves as he looks at me. "Thirty minutes. My office. The basement one."

I nod, knowing it's his office below a pizzeria. I've been there before when Niko and I were allies.

With that, Niko turns on his heel and storms out, the door slamming shut behind him. Aria lets out a shaky breath, her eyes glistening with unshed tears.

I want to hold her, but I'm not sure if she'll accept my comfort. I choose my words carefully. "I don't want to make your decisions for you, but Niko is right in that our worlds are full of danger. It's our job to keep you safe."

"There's a difference between keeping me safe and locking me away."

I take a chance, pulling her into my arms. "I understand."

She looks up at me. "Luca, you can't go."

"I must. It's only respectful. I'm in his territory. If I hope to garner his blessing, I need to comply."

Her fingers grip the lapel of my robe. "What if he kills you?"

I've always felt I knew and understood Niko. Maybe not his aversion to me, but the man he is otherwise. I don't feel he'll kill me, but I can't be sure. He is *Il Soldato della Morte*, after all.

I pull away and head to the shower.

"I'm serious, Luca. I'm worried he'll try to kill you."

"Not if I kill him first." The words are out before I can think better of them.

"Do you hear yourself? This whole thing is ridiculous. You're both going to try and kill each other because you love me. I could have two men who love me, but you're both so stupid that you'll kill each other instead."

She's right, of course. This is stupid. But it's Niko's making. I turn on the shower and drop the robe.

"Why does anyone need to kill at all? Why can't what I want matter?"

My heart aches at her words. "Aria, what you want matters more to me than anything." I go to her, abandoning the shower for the moment. "Do you want me? Do you want to return to Italy with me?"

She lets out an exasperated breath. "Yes. Of course. I just can't bear the thought of you getting hurt, or worse." Her voice cracks with emotion.

I cup her face in my hands. "I must do this, Aria. This is the only way to make things right with your brother, if that's even possible."

"What if he doesn't? What if he has some nefarious plot?"

"I'm not a coward, and I won't back down from this. But I promise you, I will do everything in my power to resolve this peacefully."

She bites her lip, her eyes searching mine. "Do you really want me, Luca? Or is this all just about power and control?"

I pull her closer, pressing my forehead to hers. "Aria, you are the only thing I want." I kiss her then, pouring all of my love and devotion into it, hoping she can feel what I can't seem to convey.

When we part, I can see the conflict in her eyes.

"I promise you, everything will be alright. I'll make sure of it." I press another kiss to her lips, then pull back. "When I'm done, we'll do something fun. Your choice."

She gives me a wan smile. I'd rather her feel reassured, but I have to deal with Niko. I step into the shower. Later when I'm dressed, I kiss her, even though she's clearly upset with me, and leave to meet Niko.

In hindsight, perhaps I should have had Bruno stay. Then again, what are two men against Niko's army?

I arrive at the pizzeria, and after checking in with one of his men, head down to his basement office. I'm not afraid to die, but I'm not ready for death. I know that I'm treading on dangerous ground. But for Aria, I'm willing to take that risk. I just hope that I can resolve this peacefully, for her sake.

I take a deep, steadying breath as I stand in front of Niko's office door. I knock firmly, squaring my shoulders.

"Come in."

I open the door, expecting a wall of Niko's men. Instead, I see Niko sitting behind his desk. I don't miss the gun resting on the desktop.

Niko leans back in his chair, his expression casual, but his eyes are like steel. "Luca. Thank you for coming."

"I wonder where your men are. Do they not support this ridiculous plot against me?"

"You flatter yourself. This isn't about you. It's about Aria and what's best for her."

We're starting off on the wrong foot. I meet his gaze as a sign of respect, not challenge. "I'm hoping to forge a peace between us."

Niko's lips curl into a humorless smile. "I'm sure you are. You nearly had my sister killed."

"I believe you are the one who told her to go to the airport without protection that left her vulnerable." I don't know this for sure except for the fact that Niko called me when Aria was missing telling me he'd expected her to be on a plane bound for the United States.

His jaw tightens.

"I also am aware that one of your own men tried to kill her, along with your pregnant wife. I believe it was Lucia who saved them. How fortunate for them that I'd allowed Lucia to make the choice to stay here."

"I can show my appreciation without handing my sister over."

I laugh. "I believe Aria handed herself over. I know she wouldn't like hearing you talk like that."

"I mean no disrespect, Luca, but my sister is to stay here."

"All you've shown me is disrespect, Niko. I'd like to know why. Give me a good reason I shouldn't marry your sister."

"I don't owe you any explanation about my decisions regarding my sister."

I hold my ground, refusing to back down. "Aria is not yours to keep. She is a grown woman, and she has made her choice. Although we don't need it, it would be nice to have your blessing."

Niko barks out a harsh laugh. "Blessing? After all this you think I'm going to bless your relationship."

"I don't care whether you do or not. But I know it would mean a lot to Aria."

"She doesn't know what she wants except maybe to drive me crazy." He shakes his head like he's said too much. "Aria is to stay in New York."

"Perhaps you should talk to Aria about this." I'm getting tired of this conversation going around and around. "Unless she changes her mind, I'm taking her home with me. Nothing is going to stop me from doing so."

Niko sneers as he picks up the gun, weighing it in his hand.

26

ARIA

I pace the hotel room frantically, my mind racing with the worst possible scenarios. It's been like this since Luca left. Now, hours later, Luca isn't answering my calls. Niko isn't either. I'm convinced something terrible has happened.

If Luca is dead, I don't know what I'll do. The thought of losing him makes my heart ache in my chest. But if Niko is the one who's gone, that too hurts. Plus, utter chaos that could erupt in New York City terrifies me. My brother is the most powerful Don on the East Coast. His death could spark a war.

I keep glancing at my phone, willing it to ring, but the silence increases my fear that one or both are gone. The thought makes me sick to my stomach. I can't lose them both. I just can't.

I collapse onto the bed, my hands trembling as I dial Elena's number. I hate to call her and make her worry, but I can no longer wait and wonder my fate.

"Hey, Aria." Elena's voice is chipper. I dread what I have to say.

"Hey. Have you heard from Niko?"

"Not since this morning. Why?"

I gnaw on my lip as I realize she must not know Niko planned to see Luca. "Did you know he came to my hotel?"

"He said something about wanting to talk to you. Why? Is something wrong?"

I consider the situation. Was Niko caught off guard at seeing Luca here? I shake my head. No. He acted like he knew he'd find Luca, which means one of his men had spotted him and called.

"I think something is wrong. I can't get ahold of Luca, and I'm so afraid something's happened to him... or Niko."

Elena's voice is immediately concerned. "Luca? What's going on?"

"He came to New York to be with me. Niko showed up demanding to see him. It wasn't a friendly exchange, and now I can't get ahold of either of them."

She's quiet, and I wish I could see her face to know what she might be thinking. "I'll try to reach Niko. Just stay put, okay? I'm sure everything is going to be fine."

I nod, even though she can't see me, and wait anxiously as she hangs up to make the call. The minutes feel like hours as I sit on the edge of the bed, my heart pounding in my chest. *Please, let them both be okay.*

Finally, my phone rings, and I scramble to answer it. "Elena?"

"Aria, Niko's on his way home," she says, her voice sounding relieved. "He's alright."

I let out a shaky breath, but the knot in my stomach doesn't loosen. "What about Luca?"

Elena's hesitation makes my heart stop. "Niko... didn't confirm anything about Luca. He just said Luca was 'dealt with'."

I feel the blood drain from my face as the implication of her words sinks in. "Oh, God," I whisper, my hand trembling as I bring it to my mouth. "Is he...?" I can't bring myself to say the words.

"I don't know. Niko didn't say that. He could have just sent Luca away, or—" She stops, and I hear one of the twins crying. "I'll talk to him when he gets home. I'm sorry, I need to go. Niko is a difficult man, but... well, I can't see him going that far. Just try to stay calm, okay? I'll let you know if I hear anything else."

The line goes dead, and I'm left sitting in the hotel room, my heart racing. Has Niko just taken the one thing that is important to me? I've lost my parents and a brother. My surviving brother sent me away. For so long, I had no one until Luca, and now Niko took that from me.

I am beyond angry. Fueled by rage and growing hate, I grab my purse and exit my room. It occurs to me that I have no protection that Niko was so adamant I needed. I don't have it because he took it from me.

I order a car and give the driver the address to Niko's penthouse. When I arrive, his men say hello to me, but I push past them.

"Is he here?"

"He just went up." One of his men presses the button for the elevator for me. As the elevator rises, so too do my fury and resentment. The elevator stops, and I step out, banging on Niko's door.

It swings open. "Aria?" Niko greets me with concern, his brow furrowed as he takes in my appearance. "You're out without protection."

"And whose fault is that?" I shove him in the chest hard. "What did you do?" I'm on the verge of weeping. Of screaming. Of going mad.

His eyes widen, taken aback by the intensity of my outburst. "Aria, what are you—"

"Don't play dumb with me!" I snarl, the words spilling out in a torrent of emotion. "I loved him, Niko. I loved him more than anything, and you took him away from me!"

Niko opens his mouth, but I cut him off, the anger coursing through me like a raging river.

"How could you do this to me? How can you still hate me so much that you'd rip the one person I've ever truly loved out of my life?"

The penthouse falls silent, save for the sound of my ragged breathing. Niko stands there, stunned. Elena appears, her expression concerned, but she doesn't say anything.

Guilt and conflict war in Niko's expression. It confirms my fears. All I can think about is Luca, his warm embrace, his tender kisses, his unwavering devotion—all of it snatched away by my own brother's hand.

I clench my fists. At this moment, I want nothing more than to wrap my hands around Niko's neck and squeeze. I want him to feel the anguish that tears at my heart.

"Why, Niko?" I whisper, my voice laced with a broken desperation. "Why did you do this to me?"

Elena's voice of reason cuts through. "You need to talk to her, Niko."

I shake my head. "Why bother? It will be more of the same. You don't know what you want, Aria. You're too naïve, Aria. I'm the boss of you, Aria. What I don't understand is why? What have I ever done to you to deserve this?"

Niko steps forward, his expression filled with remorse. "Aria, I... I'm so sorry. I never meant to—"

"Save it, Niko," I interrupt, holding up a hand. "I'm done." I turn to leave.

Elena steps in front of me. "Aria, please, just hear him out. He's trying to make amends."

I hesitate, my gaze flickering between the two of them. I'm so mad and hurt that I can't see straight.

Niko takes a deep breath. "You won't find this a fitting excuse, but when I became your guardian, I had no clue what to do. The business, I understood. Revenge, I understood. But raising a kid? And after the way Lorenzo and Mom were killed... I had to protect you from that. Sending you to school in Europe was the way to do it."

"I know. You got me out of your hair, out of your life, and forgot about me."

He looks at Elena like he needs help. She nods, urging him on.

"That's not true... I just... I didn't know how to be what you needed."

"A brother? We lost Dad, and then Lorenzo and Mom. And then I lost you."

Niko's breath hitches. Elena's eyes are filled with grief. I hate seeing it. It makes me think they didn't realize what Niko's actions did to me.

"And now you've taken Luca. God. If you don't think his men won't be coming here—"

"What are you talking about?" Niko asks.

"Luca. Remember, the man I love who loves me but that you had to take away because heaven forbid Aria Leone has love in her life."

"I didn't take Luca."

For a moment, the world stops as I try to understand what he's saying. "Then where is he? Why won't he answer the phone?"

"I don't know. We talked. Came to an impasse. And he left. He said he was going to take you back to Italy whether I blessed your relationship or not."

I stumble back, wondering what this can mean.

"But Aria…"

I glance up at him.

"I didn't realize how you felt… how you experienced all this."

My eyes narrow on him as anger fills me again. "How could you? You never ask me. You don't care how I feel. You just want me to be quiet and stay out of the way."

He closes his eyes for a moment. "That's not accurate. But I can see how you'd think that. And you're right. I don't take into consideration what you want."

"Maybe you didn't do anything, but did one of your men? Why would Luca just disappear?"

"None of my men did anything." He steps forward, putting his hand on my shoulder. I want to knock it off, but he'd see it as being imma-ture. "I know I failed you. I see it better now that I ever have, and trust me, Aria, I've carried guilt about you for a long time. I want to do right by you. You're here now. We're a family again. You, me, Elena, and the kids. I want to keep that."

I gape at him. "That's why you want to keep me away from Luca?"

He shrugs. "I lost everyone too. Following their deaths, I burned this Family down, taking over the Leone Family business. That puts you in danger. I couldn't lose you too."

His words don't make sense to me.

"You sent me away."

"But you weren't lost. I always knew what you were up to. You always seemed happy. And life here… God, until six months ago, it was a fucking bloodbath. It's not that I didn't want you here, it's just that I didn't know how else to protect you." The sincerity in his voice is soft-ening my anger even though I don't want it to.

"Luca is a good man."

He nods. "Maybe, but he wants to take you from me."

I shake my head. "That's not true. I'm here, aren't I? He didn't keep me from my family. Luca understands family better than you."

Niko looks down. "I'm sorry." He sucks in a breath. "If you love him, you can go—"

"No." I hold my finger up in his face. "You don't give me permission. I make this decision. You can be happy for me. You can support me. But you don't give me permission."

Elena's lips twitch upward. "She seems quite grown up and able to make her own decisions."

"It doesn't change that she needs protection. Whether with me or Luca, she needs—"

"I'm sure Luca will take care of it."

Yeah, if he hasn't run off. I can hardly blame him. The Leone family is nuts.

"Except he's missing," I say.

"I left him only thirty or forty minutes ago," Niko says. "He got a call. He said he needed to arrange to return to Italy."

My heart drops. Luca has given up on me. Every ounce of energy in me fades. I'm so tired.

"I swear, Aria, I didn't hurt him."

I turn to leave. "I'm going back to the hotel."

"Why don't you stay here?" Elena offers.

"I can't." I need to figure out my next step. If Luca has given up on me, where do I go from here?

My phone pings with a notification. I pull it from my purse, disinterested in what it might tell me.

How's your Italian?

I stare at the message, confused. And then it hits me. "I've got to go." With renewed energy, I head to Niko's front door.

"Let me go with you," Niko says.

"No." I exit his penthouse and poke the button to the elevator.

"I'm not joking about protection, Aria."

"Fine. Give me Danny or Marco. They know where I'm going."

Niko shakes his head. "I want to see him. That text is from Luca, right?"

I roll my eyes. "God, will you ever give it up?"

"I want to give my blessing."

Tears well in my eyes. Finally, he's coming around.

He gives a small shrug. "And promise to kill him if he hurts you."

I shake my head. "You're warped."

Moments later, we're in a car heading to the bookstore. My heart is beating a million miles a minute. What will I find there? A love note? A Dear Jane letter?

"Can you tell me what we're doing?" Niko asks. His voice is tentative, as if he knows he's treading on thin ice.

"A bookstore. Luca used to leave me notes there."

His jaw tightens and he looks out the window.

"What?" I demand.

He shrugs. "It sounds very romantic. I can see why you'd fall for him."

I narrow my eyes on him. "I fell for him before the notes. My head isn't in the clouds, Niko. I'm not a lovesick school girl. Yes, the notes are romantic, but it's more than that."

He holds his hands up in surrender. "Okay."

We arrive at the bookstore. The sight of it fills me with a bittersweet nostalgia, a reminder of the fleeting moments of joy I experienced with Luca. The familiar scent of books envelops me, transporting me back to those exciting moments when I'd come to find Luca's message.

I approach the language book section, my heart pounding in my chest. Carefully, I push aside a few Italian language books. The anticipation builds as I search the shelves, my eyes scanning every inch for any sign of a note from Luka. I hold my breath, desperate to find some sort of connection, some reassurance that he still loves me, that he hasn't abandoned me.

"What are you looking for?" Niko asks.

"The note. There must be one." Finally, I see it slipped next to a copy of *La Vita Nuova*, a book of love poems. My heart swells thinking this is a good sign. My fingers shake as I unfold the note.

Mio Angelo,

I'm sorry that I was not successful in earning Niko's blessing. My love for you never wavers, and as much as I want to steal you away, the choice must be yours.

I am forced to return to Italy tonight. My plane leaves at six. I pray you will come to me.

Should you choose to stay in New York for now or for forever, I'll understand.

Ti Amo,

Luca

I GLANCE at Niko who's trying to read the note. I clutch it to my chest. "Are you making him leave?"

Niko shakes his head. "No. I told you, he got a call. He said he had to go, and I was fine with that. We weren't getting anywhere."

"You mean you weren't able to make him leave me. Abandon me."

He winces. "I'm a fucker. That's not new information. I just... it's no excuse, but I know I've handled everything wrong since you were a girl. Now, with you back, was my chance."

I don't like what Niko did, but I see sincerity in his expression that has me leaning toward forgiving him.

"It looks like I won't have that chance." He nods toward the letter.

"Just because I'll be in Italy, doesn't mean we can't have a relationship. I'll be able to come visit—"

He scoffs. "I doubt he'll let you come."

"Again with the permission." I give him a light tap on the cheek. "I'd already talked to him about needing to have you and Elena and the babies... everyone here... in my life. He might not have liked it, but he's not as much of an asshole as you are. He wants me to be happy."

He grimaces. "I want you to be happy too."

"Then take me to the airport."

"Now? Can't you say a little longer? I haven't seen you—"

"I wasn't the one hiding."

"Fucking hell, Aria. I'm trying here."

I stop to face him. "I appreciate what you've shared with me. I know it was hard for you. And I really hope you mean it when you say you're okay with me and Luca. I want to be able to be with everyone I love, without drama and conflict. But right now, I need to go to Luca."

Niko sucks in a breath. "If he leaves at six, you don't have much time."

We exit the bookstore and get back into Niko's car, his driver taking us to the airport.

"Why not just call?" Niko asks as I reread the note.

"Because this is romantic." I shake my head. "You should try it some-time. I bet Elena would love it." I scribble a note on the back of the paper Luca left for me. Then I snap a picture of it.

"What are you doing?" Niko asks.

"I'm leaving a note." I could call or text, but this seems more roman-tic. I hit send and then cross my fingers that we make it to the airport in time.

27

LUCA

I take a deep breath, my heart pounding as I stand on the tarmac, waiting for any sign of Aria. I check my watch. In a moment, I'll have to board the plane if we're to leave on time. I'm torn about returning to Italy so quickly. But the call from Bruno telling me some of Sabini's men attacked one of my clubs means I'm needed home. A part of me wants to say fuck it and just stay in New York. Another part of me knows that doing so might put more strain on all of us. Aria is clear that she doesn't belong to me or Niko. So, she needs to make her choice again. I recall her annoyance at me as I left and wonder if I've played this all wrong.

Why can't Niko see my love for her? My meeting with Niko had been tense, as I damn near pleaded with him to give us his blessing. Instead, he toyed with his gun, as if that would scare me away. Perhaps others would be scared. He's *Il Soldato della Morte*, after all. But I know that if he killed me, he'd also kill Aria's love for him. I knew he knew it too.

But then Bruno's call came in and I was forced to make plans to return home. I second guess my decision to leave Aria a note instead of calling her directly. At the time, I wanted to remind her of the sweet romance we have. But as I wait, my watch ticking closer to six, I think I should have called. Or maybe she's changed her mind. Maybe she's tired of all this drama and angst.

Suddenly, my phone buzzes with a notification. It's a text from Aria, and my breath catches in my throat. I quickly open it, my eyes scanning a photo of a note.

I'm coming.

Relief floods through me, and a smile tugs at my lips. She's coming. She still wants to be with me.

The pilot approaches, informing me that we need to depart soon. I nod, my gaze fixed on the private entrance to the airport. Seconds feel like hours as I stand there, praying that she'll make it in time. I could postpone the flight, although the pilot already told me a delay could mean not leaving until tomorrow. I really need to get home to stop Sabini's men from burning my business to the ground.

A car zooms in, flying toward the plane and screeching to a halt nearby. Immediately, I'm on high alert at the aggressive approach. I wonder if Aria's note is a ruse. Maybe Niko sent it and this is an ambush, after all.

Instinctively, I reach for my gun, prepared for whatever he might bring.

The back passenger door opens and Aria jumps out, rushing to me. I release my gun just as she flings herself into my arms. I wrap my arms around her, holding her tightly. Her familiar scent and the warmth of her body instantly calms the anxiety I felt moments ago. I let out a shaky breath, relief washing over me.

I see Niko exit the car and move toward us. Again, I tense for what might happen. Niko's expression is unreadable, and I brace myself for the worst.

"Luca," Niko says, his voice level.

I glance down at Aria, searching her face for any sign of fear or distress. But she only looks up at me with hopeful eyes, her grip on me tightening. Sensing her reassurance, I nod and turn my attention to Niko.

"Niko."

He studies me. "Take care of my sister."

"I'm not a child," she complains.

I nod, knowing that by agreeing to take care of her when she doesn't want a caretaker would annoy her, but I want to acknowledge what Niko wants from me.

"Niko realizes what an overbearing, controlling asshole he's been."

My lips twitch upward. "Is that so?"

Niko grinds his teeth. "I want her to be happy. If that's with you, then... I give my blessing."

I'm speechless, my mind racing to process this unexpected turn of events. Aria beams up at me, her eyes shining with joy, and I can't help but pull her closer, holding her tight.

"Thank you, Niko," I say, my voice thick with emotion.

Niko nods, a small smile tugging at the corners of his mouth. I glance down at Aria, my chest filled with emotion. I decide there is no time like the present.

I drop to one knee as I pull a small box from my pocket. I want to give my angel her fairy tale. She gasps and looks at Niko with excitement.

"Aria Leone, you've captured my heart since the moment I met you. I've loved you from that first moment on. Will you marry me?"

Behind her, Niko rolls his eyes. Clearly, he's not a romantic. The excitement and love in Aria's eyes tells me she is.

She laughs. "I thought we were already getting married."

"Yes, well, that was my plan. I want to make sure that it's your plan as well. Do you choose me to be your husband?" I hold up the ring. "This was my grandmother's and then my mother's. I want you to have it, Aria, as a symbol of my love and my commitment to you."

Aria's eyes glisten with unshed tears as she holds out her hand, allowing me to slide the ring onto her delicate finger. "Yes, yes... of course, I'll marry you!"

Overcome with joy, I pull her into my arms, holding her tightly. In that moment, nothing else matters—not the conflict with Niko, not the dangers of the Mafia world. All that exists are Aria and the promise of a future we'll build together.

As I reluctantly release her, I turn to face Niko, bracing myself for his reaction. To my surprise, his expression is not one of anger, but of... acceptance? He steps forward and envelops Aria in a tight embrace, whispering something in her ear that I can't quite make out.

When he finally releases her, Niko turns to me, his gaze intense. "Congratulations."

"Thank you."

"You're a dead man if you hurt her."

"That goes without saying."

Niko extends his hand, and I grasp it firmly, sealing the unspoken truce between us. At that moment, I know that Aria's happiness is the only thing that matters to both of us.

I pull Aria close, my heart swelling with joy and relief. "Ready to go home?"

Aria nods, a radiant smile lighting up her face. "Yes."

We say our goodbyes to Niko and board the plane. The minute we're airborne, I tug Aria into my lap. "Did your brother hit his head?"

She laughs. "Yes, I whopped him."

I snort.

"I don't know what specifically changed his mind." Aria runs her finger through my hair, her expression thoughtful. "He said that he didn't know how to be a good brother when I was younger. Maybe I should have realized how difficult it was for him to lose everyone in our family by the time he was twenty. He was so filled with hate and revenge. He sent me away, and it felt like to me he didn't want me around. He says it was that he didn't know how to do anything but protect me." She inhales a breath. "I should have figured that out. His life's goal was power and revenge. Until Elena, I didn't know he had a soft spot deep in his heart."

"But in doing so, he wasn't looking out for your heart." I press my hand on her chest, not in a sexual gesture, but to feel the beat of her heart. A heart that beats for me.

She nods. "I felt abandoned. I'd lost my parents and other brother, and then he shipped me off, losing him too. He says he did it because he couldn't lose me, which doesn't make sense."

"I don't know. If the only way I knew I could keep you safe was to send you away, I'd do it in a minute. I know you don't like me talking like that, but it is what it is."

"Mafia men can be so exasperating."

I grin at her. "But sexy too, right?"

She laughs. "Sexy too."

I tilt my head. "So it's not me, per se, that was the problem?"

"No, except you're in Italy. I think he realized how much we missed of each other's lives and wanted to make up for it. That's easier if I'm in New York. You're taking away his chance to make things right. Or so he sees it. Did I ever mention he's a bit dense?"

I smile. "Niko is a smart man. He loves his family, even if he's dense sometimes."

"Yeah, well he finally decided that my happiness was worth considering in his calculations. Not that he has any say." She looks at me in earnest. "I know his blessing means a lot, but I don't need his permission."

I nod. "His approval means something to me, *Mio Angelo*. But your love is the most important thing."

Aria's lips curve into a tender smile. "I do love you, Luca." She leans in, pressing a soft kiss to my lips. "This is where I want to be. You're the one I choose."

I return her kiss, my arms tightening around her. She shifts on my lap, and immediately, a kiss that is just about love morphs into a physical need.

She lifts her head, her eyes sparkling. "Is that another gift I feel?" She shifts again.

"I have a new experience for you," I say as I stand and carry her back to the small bedroom on the plane.

"Ooh, I like the sound of that." She loops her arms around my neck. "The Mile High Club."

"Would you like to join?"

"Only if you initiate me."

My dick is throbbing in my slacks, ready to do just that. But I want to do more than fuck her. I want to make love. I want to touch and taste every inch of her. I want her to feel so fucking good.

I strip her bare and lay her on the bed. I remove my clothes and then climb over her, lying on her and kissing her as my hands roam. I can feel her go soft and pliant. That's when I slow things down and explore her body. I trail kisses down her neck as I knead her tits. I move down until I can wrap my lips around her hard nipples and suck. I settle in, loving how she sighs and mewls. The way her body rocks under me simply from sucking her nipples.

"Luca." Her voice is desperate. Her hand wraps around my cock, tugging as she tries to move until I can enter her.

"Relax, *Mio Angelo*." I run my fingers down her stomach, through her soft folds. I circle her clit. "This is a long ceremony. You'll come so many times."

She arches and moans. I insert one finger, then two as I trail my lips lower, lower.

"Oh, God... Luca." Her hips rock, fucking my fingers. I lick her clit, and she hisses. Finally, I suck her clit as I finger her, reaching that one spot that always makes women come.

She cries out, her body bowing off the bed. I continue to finger fuck her and play with her clit until she's coming again and again. Only when I sense she's hit her limit do I stop. My caress is gentle, as are my kisses, as I continue down her body, sucking on her inner thigh, leaving a mark. She'd hate the idea that I've branded her mine, so I don't mention it.

I move back up, still taking my time, tasting, touching, searing her essence into my brain. When I'm ninety years old suffering from dementia, I'll still remember this. Remember all of Aria.

I lie over her again, kissing her sweetly, tenderly. "*Ti amo, Mio Angelo*."

"*Ti amo*," she says as her breath comes back to her.

I position myself at her entrance as I take her hands, lacing my fingers through hers. "*Guardami*. Look at me."

Her eyes flutter open. God, they're so beautiful. I press my hips down and up, slowly, oh, so fucking slowly, entering her, joining with her. Her cheeks are flushed in a lovely pink hue. Her dark eyes watch me. I see so much love in them. More love than I deserve. I vow to always try harder to be worthy of her love.

Her legs wrap around my hips and hold me seeped inside her. I dip my head and kiss her. Our bodies are one, a single heart and soul. The emotion of it is so brutally raw and pure.

I want to stay like this forever, but nature has other ideas. My body slowly rocks, the friction building and building until our dance is fast, furious, glorious. Together we rise, reaching the pinnacle.

"Luca!" She cries out, her hands gripping mine as hard as her pussy grips my dick.

Stars burst behind my eyes as pleasure floods my body. "Yes, baby... yes..." I pump in and out, my essence filling her. An image of her ripe and round with our child flashes in my mind. I wonder how long she'll want to wait before we have children. But first a wedding... inwardly, I laugh at how eager I am for my full life with Aria to begin.

But it has begun, I realize as I roll to my side and pull her next to me. It started the moment she showed up at the plane. With or without Niko's blessing, her choice this time, knowing all that she knows about me, was the moment my heart started beating. When life filled my soul.

EPILOGUE I

Aria – Two Weeks Later

Fairy tales are fiction, but if they were true, my life would be one. Since returning to Italy with Luca, happiness surrounds me. Not that there aren't moments of tension. Sometimes, Luca oversteps in his demands or tone. But I'm strong enough to stand up for myself instead of second guessing and running away.

And now... today... will be the happiest day of my life so far.

I take a deep breath as I stand in the little room in the cathedral, the same one where Luca's parents were married years ago. The ornate, vaulted ceilings and stained-glass windows fill me with a sense of awe and reverence. This is the moment I've been dreaming of, marrying the man I love.

My heart flutters with excitement as I look around at the familiar faces gathered here today. Lucy, heavily pregnant, fusses over my dress, making sure every detail is perfect. Elena helps me with my makeup. Kate assists in putting on my headpiece and veil.

Roberta and Lia enter, juggling Elena and Kate's babies as they make their way toward us. Lia beams at me, her eyes shining with happiness. Roberta nods. She works for Luca, but her expression hints at the stronger bond she feels for him.

I feel so fortunate to have all my loved ones here to witness this momentous occasion. The last few months have been a whirlwind, filled with challenges and uncertainty. But standing here, surrounded by the people who mean the most to me, I know that I'm exactly where I'm supposed to be.

I glance over at Lucy as she sits and fans herself, the late summer heat clearly taking a toll on her.

She's heavily pregnant, her belly protruding like a round ball. "Ugh, I don't know how much longer I can last in this heat," she grumbles, wiping the perspiration from her brow. "If this baby decides to come early, I swear—"

"Don't say such a thing," Elena interrupts. "Don't tempt fate."

I try to reassure myself that the doctor is on hand, just in case. But the thought of Lucy going into labor prematurely has my stomach in knots. She has eight weeks left, and her doctor okayed the trip as long as she took specific precautions.

Roberta hands Lucy a glass of water and speaks to her in Italian. Admittedly, I'm still a long way from fluent, so I'm not sure of the conversation. But I see a similar reverence in Roberta's eyes for Lucy that she has for Luca. I've learned that while Lucy can be a kickass woman, here, they love her for how well she took care of Luca's father.

I'm filled with giddy anticipation. In just a few moments, I'll walk down the aisle to join my life with Luca's. The very thought of him has my heart racing with equal parts excitement and nervousness.

The door to the little room off the vestibule opens, and Niko strides in, a warm smile on his face. It's not something I've seen a lot in my life, but more so since we talked. In the last two weeks, we spoke more via video call, often reminiscing about our lives before we lost everyone but each other.

"You look beautiful, Aria."

"Thank you." I sniff as emotion wells in my chest.

"Are you ready?"

I take a deep breath and nod. "I am."

Elena gives me a hug. "Luca is going to weep with joy when he sees you."

Kate follows with another hug. "I'm so happy for you."

Finally, Lucy gives me a side hug. "Sorry I can't give you a full one, but this little person needs space." She kisses me on the cheek. "I know Luca's father would think the world of you and thank you personally for making his son happy."

Her words fill me with more emotion.

"Giuseppe always said that the right woman was the source of a man's power. Remember that." She winks, and I laugh, understanding that she's encouraging me to continue to be myself and make my own choices.

The ladies leave, followed by Roberta and Lia with the kids. I'm left with just Niko.

His expression softens as he reaches into his pocket, pulling out a rectangle box. "Before we go, I have something for you."

I watch, transfixed, as he opens the box to reveal a stunning pearl necklace and matching earrings. "These were Mother's," he says, his voice thick with emotion. "I've been saving them for you."

Tears spring to my eyes as I gently trace the intricate design of the necklace. I'm scanning my memory with her wearing them. I remember once sneaking up late at night when my parents got home from some party. I saw them dancing, my father singing in Italian to my mother. That was the first time I saw true love. She wore these pieces then.

"I know she'd love if you wore them. Have a piece of her with you."

I sniff, unable to find words.

"And this." He tugs a blue handkerchief from his pocket. "It was Dad's. I know it's worn, but it's old and blue."

"And he can be here too." I wait, knowing there must be one more thing. He takes out a picture of Lorenzo. I kiss it and slip it in my dress's pocket along with the handkerchief.

"Now you're all here."

Niko hugs me. "I hope you're as happy as you look."

"I am," I assure him.

"Because if Luca—"

I press my fingers over his lips. "You don't have to worry about me."

He smiles and nods.

I throw my arms around him, holding him tightly. Niko may not have always understood me, but he's here now, supporting me on the most important day of my life.

Niko pulls back, his eyes glistening. "Shall we?" He offers me his arm.

I entwine my arm with his. "I'm ready."

With Niko by my side, I turn toward the ornate cathedral doors, my heart pounding in anticipation. They open. I'm vaguely aware of our friends and family in the small church. But all I really see is Luca, standing at the altar in his dark suit looking so handsome. He sees me, his breath hitching. He looks at me like I'm the center of his world. I hope I can keep him looking at me like that for the rest of our lives.

I grip Niko's arm tightly as we make our way down the aisle, my gaze fixed on Luca. As Niko hands me off to Luca, I feel a sense of peace wash over me. I know in my heart that this is where I'm meant to be. Where I was always meant to be.

Luca's strong hands envelop mine. "You're absolutely breathtaking. An angel come to save me."

"And you look incredibly handsome," I whisper back.

The priest begins the ceremony, but I can barely focus on the words. All I can see is Luca, his eyes shining with love and devotion. During the vows, we commit our lives to each other forever.

Tears glisten in Luca's eyes as he slips the delicate gold band onto my finger. My vision is blurred from tears as well as I slide the gold band on his finger.

"Don't ever take this off," I add at the end, a little reminder about the discussion we had when he wasn't sure he wanted to wear a ring. All I had to say was "Electra" and he understood that it was important to me that other women could see he was taken. Sure, many women wouldn't care. Many men wouldn't honor the symbol. But Luca will. I know it as sure as I'm standing here committing my life to his.

He winks, letting me know he got the message.

The priest pronounces us husband and wife, and Luca pulls me close, his lips finding mine in a passionate, loving kiss. The world around us fades away, and in this moment, it's just the two of us, finally united as one.

When we finally break apart, breathless and giddy, Luca grins down at me. "I'm yours now, *Mio Angelo*."

"That's *Mio Angelo Conte* to you."

He lets out a wonderful laugh and kisses me again. "Ready to make our grand exit, Mrs. Conte?"

"Ready when you are."

He surprises me by swooping me up in his arms and carrying me down the aisle. I see Donovan patting Niko on the back and giving Luca a thumbs up. Even serious Liam is smiling, his arm around Kate as she holds their daughter.

As we reach the car, Luca presses a fervent kiss to my lips. "I've been waiting for this day since I met you."

I wrap my arms around his neck. "And now we have forever."

With one last, lingering kiss, we tumble into the car, our hearts racing with excitement as we embark on the next chapter of our lives. I don't know what the future holds. I'm certain of happiness, but I'm not so naïve to believe we won't face challenges. But I know for sure, the one constant will be our love. We'll get through whatever life throws at us together.

And I'm right. The next six months have been a whirlwind of wedded bliss. Luca and I have settled into a comfortable routine in our villa along the Italian coast. Each day, I find myself falling more deeply in love with my husband and the life we've built together.

My Italian has improved by leaps and bounds, thanks to the patient tutelage of Lia over the summer, and Bianca and the wives' help thereafter. Luca delights in hearing me converse with the staff and locals, his eyes shining with pride. Late at night, he often shares with me not safe for work conversations that involve our getting naked. I like those lessons the best, even if I can't use the words outside our bedroom.

We've had the chance to visit New York twice since our wedding. The first trip was to meet Lucia and Donovan's newborn son, Giuseppe, after Luca's father. Luca was beyond touched by their choice.

During that trip, I doted on my niece and nephew, amazed at how fast they were growing. It wouldn't be long before I'd be able to take little Angelica shopping. I'll bring Kate and Liam's daughter, Sophie, with me as well.

Niko seemed genuinely happy to see me, his gruff exterior softening as he watched me with Luca. It felt good to have my brother's blessing, even if the road to get here was fraught with challenges.

Our second visit was for Christmas, and I was overjoyed to be surrounded by my loved ones once more. On that visit, it was decided that the Christmas tradition would be to spend it all together in Niko and Elena's Long Island compound.

Today, spring is working its way in and I sit on the villa terrace enjoying the warming weather and view of the ocean. I'm waiting for Luca to arrive home from his meeting with Bruno that will include Rocco. I'm curious to find out about Electra, who had her baby two months ago.

The door to the terrace opens, and I can't help but smile as happiness fills me.

"What's this?" Luca says, coming to sit next to me on the loveseat. He holds up an Italian language book with a note peeking out of the top. I'd left it for him on his desk.

"You should read it and find out."

He leans in and kisses me. Then he plucks the note out of the book and opens it. His gaze immediately swings to me. "Is this... does this...?"

I look at the paper. "*Ciao, Papi.*"

"Aria." His breath hitches as he presses his palm to my cheek. "*Dimmi.*" Tell me.

"It means 'hello, Daddy.'" My head bobs up and down to confirm it means what he thinks it does. "It means you're going to be a daddy."

"Oh, *Dio*." He tugs me in, holding me so tightly I don't think he'll ever let go. That's fine with me. In Luca's arms is the only place I want to be.

His hand slides down over my belly. "It happened fast."

I laugh. It's true. We decided only a few weeks ago to start our family. "It's all that potent sperm you have."

His cheeks blush. "My fertile wife." He kisses me softly. "*Mio Angelo*." My angel. It's one of the many pet names he has for me. All of them tell me how much he loves and cherishes me. Sometimes, I'm surprised at how unsure I was when I first came to him. But now I understand that it was about me and needing to find my footing.

Now, I have no doubts. No matter the challenges, we are one heart. One soul. Forever and ever.

EPILOGUE II

Luca – Two Years Later

I sit on the floor of Niko and Elena's Long Island mansion at the base of a Christmas tree watching my son, Teodoro, or Teddy, as Aria likes to call him. He's about to turn one in January. I can't believe how big he's grown in the last twelve months. To see him emerge so tiny and delicate from Aria's body, it was like a miracle. Even now, I find it hard to believe that a man like me could be allowed to witness such beauty.

Today, he's twenty-three pounds of sturdy boy. The kid is walking, falling, bumping, rolling into everything. He's the delight of my life. Right there with Aria. She's sitting on the couch watching me and Teddy. I wink at her and wonder if it's too soon to pitch a second child.

"What is it about kids that they like the packaging more than the toy?" Lucia ponders as she watches her two-year-old son, Giuseppe, kick balled up wrapping paper around the room with the help of his father, Donovan.

"I like toys." Niccola, Niko and Elena's three-year-old son, is pushing a car around the room. His sister, Angelica, is sitting in Niko's lap as they look at a picture book.

Three years ago, if someone had said I'd be in this place, with these people, with a wife and son, I'd have called them *pazzo*, crazy. Yet here I am, and I'm so fucking glad to be here.

We arrived two days ago and have been staying at a penthouse we bought last year for when we come to visit, or when Aria wants to shop and see her friends on a whim. We'll stay through New Years and get home by January sixth to celebrate *Epifania*. In Italy, our Christmas season starts December eighth and runs through January sixth, something Aria was pretty excited to learn about.

A knock sounds on Niko's door, and Liam and Kate enter.

Their two-year-old girl squirms to get out of Liam's arms. "Play!"

Liam sets her down with a laugh. It's still a shock to me when he cracks a smile. I didn't know him well before, but when I had the opportunity to be around him when Lucia was battling her father, he always seemed so grim and serious. Aria tells me that's what the love of a good woman can do for a man. It makes me think of my father and his belief that a good woman is a man's source of power. I suppose Liam proves that. Aria proves it with me.

"Dinner is ready," Elena calls to all of us.

Aria shows up too from helping Elena and takes Teddy. As I follow them, Niko steps up beside me.

"Just thought you'd want to know, that import is all set."

I nod. "Good."

"No business," Aria and Elena say in sync. But Aria is smiling. She's happy that Niko and I don't just have a truce, but we're now in business together.

Moments later, we're around a large table. Eight adults and five children. It's noisy, but in a good way, filled with laughter and joy.

Growing up, my family was close, but my mother died when I was young, and much of the life in the villa died with her. Aria has brought that back to me. Now I have a large family. My business is thriving. My enemies are subdued at the moment. I attribute all of it to Aria, who saved me from a life without love and laughter. She's my angel.

Later that night, Teddy is in bed, and Aria and I are exhausted in the happy way that holidays bring.

"Merry Christmas, *Mio Angelo*," I say as I pull her close.

"Merry Christmas, *mio* sexy man." Her hand slides down and cups my dick. All of a sudden, I'm not so tired. "I have one more package I want to unwrap."

My dick is at full attention. "It's all yours."

We undress, and she climbs over me, straddling me. "Is it too soon to make another baby?" I ask.

She laughs as she settles her pussy over my cock. For a moment, I can't focus.

"It's not too soon, but there is an issue with making another baby."

My hands go to her hips, holding her still as concern fills me. "An issue?"

She takes my hands and presses them over her tits. Instinctively, I squeeze. "The issue is that you've already knocked me up again, *Papi*."

It takes a moment for her words to sink in.

She laughs. "We're crazy. Two kids under the age of two?"

"Niko and Elena did it." Granted, they had twins, but still.

She leans over, her tits brushing on my chest. "Don't talk about my brother while I'm having sex with you. It ruins the mood."

I roll her under me, pulling her thigh up, opening her more and sliding in deeper. "Tell me what you want, Signora Conte."

Her eyes flash with heat. "Fuck me, Don Conte." She repeats it in Italian. It winds me up, and I start to move.

As we reach the end game, she presses her hands to my cheeks. "*Ti amo*, Luca."

The emotion floods through me like a tidal wave, making the moment even sweeter, sexier. I buck as my orgasm sweeps through me, and through her. We're one in a dance all our own, our bodies, our souls entwined. It's fucking perfection.

"*Ti amo, Mio Angelo.*" My angel of mercy.

Loved Luca and Aria? Great News! **The entire Shadows of Redemption series is now available for your reading pleasure.**

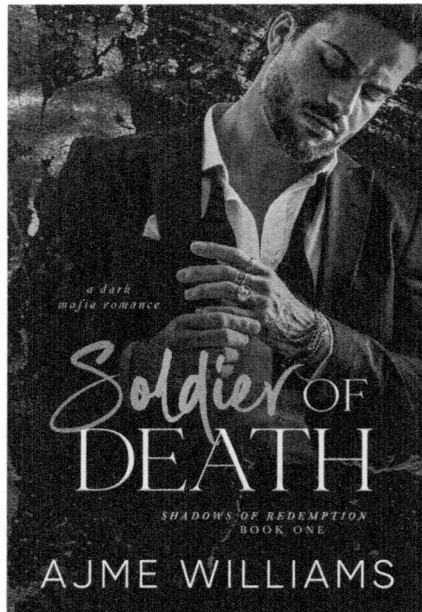

Soldier of Death (Niko and Elena)

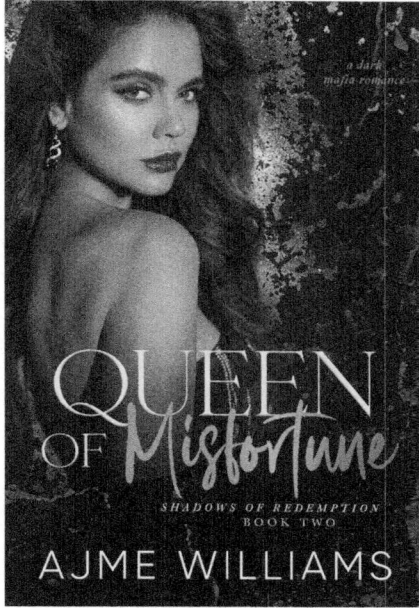

Queen of Misfortune (Donovan and Lucy)

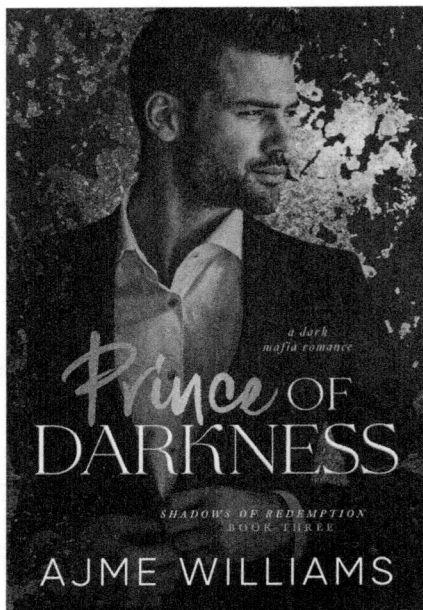

Prince of Darkness (Liam and Kate)

WANT MORE AJME WILLIAMS?

Join my no spam mailing list here.

You'll only be sent emails about my new releases, extended epilogues, deleted scenes and occasional FREE books.

Printed in Great Britain
by Amazon